HEART OF MY HEART
Stella MacLean

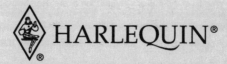

HARLEQUIN®

TORONTO • NEW YORK • LONDON
AMSTERDAM • PARIS • SYDNEY • HAMBURG
STOCKHOLM • ATHENS • TOKYO • MILAN • MADRID
PRAGUE • WARSAW • BUDAPEST • AUCKLAND

ISBN-13: 978-0-373-78232-1
ISBN-10:   0-373-78232-2

HEART OF MY HEART

ABOUT THE AUTHOR

Stella MacLean has spent her life collecting story ideas, waiting for the day someone would want to read about the characters who have lurked in her heart and mind for so many years. Stella's love of reading and writing began in grade school and has continued to play a major role in her life. A longtime member of Romance Writers of America and a Golden Heart finalist, Stella enjoys the hours she spends tucked away in her office with her Maine coon cat, Emma Jean, and her imaginary friends while writing stories about love, life and happiness. This is her first published book.

For my sister Elizabeth
and all the moments we shared.

Acknowledgments:

To Paula Eykelhof, my editor, for her
encouragement and support. To Tory, Georgie and
Julianne, who have been around since the dawn
of my ambition. But most of all, to my husband,
Garry, who knows what it's like to hear the frantic
clack of computer keys in the early-morning hours.

PROLOGUE

Olivia touched James's lips, her fingers lingering.

"I'm right here, honey, and everything's going to be just fine," she whispered, smiling at him as her mind rushed back forty years to the moment when she'd first known that she and James might share a future….

She'd come out of her high school basketball practice, her damp hair clinging to her face. She wasn't looking forward to the long walk home along the dark streets of Frampton, but there wasn't any choice.

Holding her books between her knees while she clipped her unruly hair out of the way, she'd heard someone approaching. From the end of the corridor, where only a red emergency exit light burned, a form had appeared.

His long-legged stride brought James McElroy into view, and Olivia gasped in surprise. She'd straightened, grabbing her books as she did. "Hi," she said, knowing she probably sounded young and completely silly. Aware of how messy she must look in the tartan skirt and twin sweater set she'd worn all day, Olivia smiled to cover her unease.

"Hi, yourself," James said, coming to stand in front of her, his tall, angular frame offering just the kind of protection Olivia needed on such a dark night.

"What are you doing here?" she asked. Her words seemed so demanding to her own ears. Would he think she was being too pushy?

He smiled back at her, and it was as if someone had suddenly turned on all the lights. "Would you like a ride home?" he asked, looking at her intently....

"Darling," she asked now, "do you remember how awkward I was that first night, when you asked me if I wanted a drive?" She let her fingers trail over his brow, feeling the coolness of his skin.

"And then, when we got to your car, I was so eager to get in that I pulled on the handle before you'd unlocked the door. Talk about feeling dumb," she murmured, recalling the way his arm had slipped around her as he put the key in the lock.

"You'd planned it all along, hadn't you?" she said, her body reliving the warmth of his presence as they drove down the street toward her home near the railway tracks.

She studied his still-handsome face, only inches from hers, and all she could think about was the way he'd smiled at her that night, the way he'd teased her about her lab experiment gone wrong.

"Darling, do you remember the first time you kissed me?"

She remembered only too well.

Not knowing why the heartthrob of her high school class had offered her a ride home, she'd sat huddled close to the door of his Ford Mustang. When he'd turned into her driveway, she'd resisted the urge to slide down in the seat, away from her mother's searching gaze. Edwina Banks would be watching and waiting for her only child. There was no way in the world her mother hadn't seen James's shiny red car.

"It was the same night you asked me if I'd go with you to the St. Patrick's Day dance. I was so surprised and delighted I leaned across the seat and you kissed me."

Her fingers smoothed the skin on the back of his hand, remembering how strong his hand had felt that night when he pulled her into his arms and kissed her so gently she thought she might just float away. She would never forget the way her heart had leaped in her chest....

"'Will you go to the dance with me?' you asked, and I said I would. I don't think I ever told you this, but I spent hours finding the perfect dress to wear to that dance. I finally convinced Mom and Dad to take me shopping in Boston. It seems so ridiculous now, but back then I wanted you to be proud of me.

"Remember our little poem?" she whispered near his ear. "'If you love me as I love you, nothing but death can part us two…' Oh please, God," she sobbed, clinging to his hand as she slid down into the chair next to his bed.

Years ago, she'd uttered the words of the poem without knowing the pain of them. Yet in this moment of anguish, she faced the raw truth—she would promise *anything,* make any sacrifice, give up everything, if only he'd get better.

The door opened. Olivia turned; her fingers squeezed the soft flesh of his hand.

"The doctor will see you now," the nurse said, her gaze at once gentle and analytical.

Not wanting to leave her husband, but aware of the nurse waiting at the door, Olivia squared her shoulders and rose from the chair. "I'll be back as soon as I can," she promised, easing her fingers from his.

The cool tones of the overhead lighting added to her sense of unreality as she matched the nurse's purposeful stride. They left the Intensive Care unit and when she glanced across the hospital corridor toward the double doors that led to the operating room, fear welled up in her.

During the long hours while James was in surgery, Olivia gave up counting the number of times the overhead paging system had issued an urgent message, the times people pushing carts and stretchers had passed her by, their attention focused on some urgent rendezvous beyond the doors. She'd given up counting the number of times her lips moved in prayer for the one person behind those doors who mattered to her.

Think positive, she murmured to herself. James was going to make it. He had to. James had always confronted life without fear.

"In here, Mrs. McElroy," the nurse said, pointing to a room and a man she'd met only hours before.

"Please come in," Dr. Crealock said, extending his hand in welcome.

"Is James okay?" Olivia blurted.

"Your husband is doing as well as can be expected."

Olivia didn't think he was doing well at all. She'd spent the last little while talking to him, and he hadn't stirred, nor had he acknowledged her.

"I need to know what to tell my son when he calls back. I want him to be here."

"That's a good idea, Mrs. McElroy, because

the surgery was more problematic than we expected. James developed a complication involving a clotting problem. It would be advisable for you to get the other members of his family here as soon as possible."

Olivia's knees refused to hold her, and she sank into the nearest chair, a strange lightness filling her head. God help her, she was going to faint. Grabbing the arm of the chair, she lowered her head.

"I'm sorry to upset you," the doctor said, kneeling in front of her as he spoke, his voice consoling.

The genuine sympathy she saw in his eyes scared her more than all the hours of waiting, more than the terrifying hours of uncertainty. "When will he be able to talk to me?"

"Not for a couple of hours. Are you going to be all right?"

What an idiotic question! With the man she loved in danger of dying, how could she be all right? If anything happened to James…

"Can I stay here for a while?"

"Yes, by all means. The nurse will come and find you when you can see your husband again. Do you need anything?"

She needed her life back. She needed to hold James in her arms, to hear his reassuring words. She needed to believe that her life would be whole again. "No, thank you."

Relief visible on his face, the young doctor patted her hands, now folded in her lap. "If there's anything we can do, please let the nurses know." Dr. Crealock eased back on his heels and stood up. "Have you got a friend you could call to come and stay with you?"

Millie Rayworth had called and offered to sit with her, but Olivia couldn't bring herself to field all the questions Millie would ask. Her friend meant well, but Olivia needed time to herself. Time to relive all the memories.

"I'll be okay. Thank you for your help."

"If you want to talk to me, just ask a nurse to page me," he said. With that, he slipped out of the room, the squeak of his rubber-soled shoes echoing with every step.

Olivia leaned back in the chair, letting the quietness of the room shield her from the painful reality of these past hours.

Hours filled with love and fear in equal measure. James McElroy was her life. And always had been.

CHAPTER ONE

Forty years earlier

OLIVIA BREATHED in the glorious scent of freshly cut lilacs—armloads of them in a corner of the gymnasium. Tiny lights glittered along the edge of the stage, over the doors and windows, and the basketball hoops were draped with purple and yellow bunting, the Frampton High colors.

Olivia smiled in contentment as she and James placed stubby candles nestled in glass pots on each of the white-clad tables that ringed the large area. James McElroy hadn't left her side all day, and she gloried in the idea that now he was truly hers.

"Whew! That's it, I guess. I'm glad to be finished, aren't you?" she asked, not the least bit glad. She cherished every moment she spent with James.

"Don't wish your life away," James teased, taking the last of the candles from her hands and setting them on a nearby table.

The sounds of the room faded as James reached

for her. "Every time I see that look in your eyes…" he murmured, pulling her behind a huge potted rubber tree and kissing her.

"Be careful," she whispered. Tingling heat charged down her spine. She wanted him to kiss her again, to claim her the way he had last night.

"Or what?" James eyed her, his smile issuing a challenge as he nestled her closer. She breathed in the scent of his Old Spice cologne. His powerful hands slid down over her waist toward her bottom, his touch suggestive.

Her cheeks flamed, and she dropped her gaze. They'd gone all the way last night. He'd been loving and gentle, although she'd been terrified. It had hurt a little, but she'd never admit that to a living soul. It was what James wanted and she'd wanted it, too. Everything would be all right. James loved her.

Everything would be perfect.

They were both headed to Hastings College after graduation. When James graduated, he'd go to work for his father, and so would she. Olivia had been awarded the first full scholarship ever given to a woman in the marketing program at Hastings. Much to her embarrassment, her parents told all her relatives at the family reunion about their only child's plans for the future.

High-pitched laughter invaded the private space

between them, making Olivia self-conscious that someone might see them. What would people think if they knew what she and James had done in the backseat of his Ford Mustang last night?

She hated herself for worrying about what people thought. If only she didn't know how much her classmates gossiped over girls who slept around. She'd heard those same girls brag about what they'd done, while she'd always harbored her mother's belief that it was wrong to have sex before marriage. Yet, deep inside, Olivia was thrilled to be part of the inner circle of girls who'd had sex with their boyfriends.

She and James had waited to be sure about their feelings. He'd given her his class ring; it would do, he'd said, until he could afford to buy her a diamond.

After last night, he'd been so attentive, so sweet. And even though he'd told her over and over how much he loved her, she still found it hard to believe. "You didn't have to stay and help me with all this."

"Where else would I be?" he asked, a mock frown creasing the smoothness of his forehead.

All her doubts faded as she smiled up at him. James and she were meant to be together; she'd known it from the very first time they'd spoken. That short drive to her house after basketball practice had changed her life.

"I wouldn't want you to be anywhere else,

either," she whispered, sliding her fingers along the cleft of his chin.

He raised her face to meet his gaze, his fingers featherlight against her skin. His hands swept up her back, toward the hook of her lace bra. "Last night was great."

It had all happened so fast, so unexpectedly, that they hadn't had a chance to think about birth control. "Last night—"

"Last night was everything I've ever wanted," James whispered in her ear.

"It was?" she whispered back, entwining her arms around his neck. Forgetting all her mother's warnings about not leading a guy on, Olivia pressed her body into his.

His pelvis strained against hers, his erection warm against the hollow of her belly. "It was. And we'll be careful, I promise. I went to the drugstore this morning."

"Oh, James, maybe we should've waited. I *can't* get pregnant."

"Trust me. You won't. And besides, you wouldn't make me suffer like this, would you?" He nuzzled her cheek, setting up a steady hum of need within her.

"I'm not sure," she teased.

"I am," he murmured, knitting his fingers into her hair.

"Easy for you to say." She gave him a playful shove as she smiled into his gloriously blue eyes with their fringe of dark lashes.

"There'll never be anyone for me but you." His thumb slipped under the gold chain that held his class ring between her breasts. "You'll always be part of my life," he said, his voice a warm caress against her cheek.

"I love you," Olivia whispered.

"I love you, too. So much." He held her gently, his kiss whisking the air from her lungs.

In that one moment, Olivia realized she'd never love anyone the way she loved James.

Abruptly, his lips left hers. "Damn! I forgot. Dad wants me to meet him at the house around six. He said it was urgent. I know we planned to go to Walden's Lodge for dinner before the dance, but I won't be able to make it. I'm sorry."

Disappointment clouded her happiness. She wanted to go with him to the restaurant, to be seen with the president of the senior class. She was so proud of him, of them. But there'd be other dinners at fine restaurants.

"I guess it's all right. We could go to the lake and watch the moon rise."

"That's not the only thing that's going to rise." He gave her a cheeky grin. "I'll get my penguin suit on and pick you up around seven."

"Better yet, why don't you meet me here? Emma's a little anxious about tonight. This is her first official event as head of the social committee."

"Olivia Banks, lady with responsibilities, comes to the rescue one more time."

"You got it."

"See you later, alligator," James said. He kissed her fingers before striding across the room toward the exit.

OLIVIA FIDDLED with the beaded strap on her evening bag as she glanced around at her classmates, who were standing in small groups, their voices tight with excitement.

"Doesn't everyone look great?" Emma Lawlor said, her enthusiasm evident in the way she clasped and unclasped her hands.

"Yes, and you did a wonderful job decorating the gym for tonight," Olivia said, meaning every word.

Despite the small complication with James's father, Olivia was sure tonight would be everything she could ever wish for. She pictured James in his tuxedo, his arm circling her waist as he led her onto the dance floor. He was so handsome, and they had such plans for tonight after the prom. She would have him all to herself in the moonlight.

If he ever got here. Not wanting to appear anxious, she resisted the urge to let her gaze search the gym. *Where was James?* The music would start any minute, and she wanted to dance the first waltz with him. Olivia loved the way James danced so close she could feel the beating of his heart.

Feeling conspicuous, Olivia gave in to the urge and looked quickly around, hoping to see someone in the same predicament. Coming through the doors of the gymnasium just then was her best friend, Grace Underhill. Relief whipping through her, Olivia hurried across the floor.

Doug Fields was walking beside Grace, a goofy grin on his face, his hair slicked down. Doug Fields was Grace's date for the senior prom? Grace, the single most beautiful girl in her graduating class, wouldn't be caught dead with someone like Doug. It didn't make sense. Doug the slug he was called, and for good reason. He was the last person in the whole of Frampton High that Grace would've dated.

Olivia never quite understood how she and Grace had become best friends. They played volleyball and basketball together, but it wasn't until they won the volleyball championship that their friendship really grew.

The Underhills had money and power and the second-biggest house in the town. Although Grace had an older brother, Mr. Underhill constantly lavished gifts and attention on Grace.

Unlike Grace's family, Olivia and her parents lived just off Main Street in a tiny Cape Cod-style house. Her dad worked for McElroy Manufacturing, which was owned by James's father, Thomas, while Grace's dad was the head accountant.

Grace floated toward Olivia, the long taffeta folds of her emerald-green skirt undulating around her hips as she walked. Her strawberry-blonde hair was held high on her head with mother-of-pearl combs and a long strand of pearls stood out against the backdrop of her clear white skin, making her plunging neckline seem even more revealing.

"Wow. What a dress."

"You like it?" Grace twirled around, nearly bumping into Doug.

"You look so sexy," Olivia said, giving Grace a heartfelt hug of welcome.

"Thanks. I needed to hear that. I have something to prove tonight. And what about you? You're gorgeous. Blue velvet brings out the gold highlights in your hair," Grace said, returning the hug.

"Where's Barry?" Olivia whispered.

"Major fight. I'll explain later." Grace glanced around. "Where's James?"

"With his dad. Some big discussion that couldn't wait."

"Wow. What do you suppose is going on? It's not like James to miss a party."

"No kidding!" Olivia tried to shrug off Grace's words.

"Looks like we both need a little consoling. Meet me at Bennie's for a soda tomorrow morning at ten and give me all the details, and I'll tell you what that snake in the grass, Barry, did," Grace said.

How could Grace be so calm about Barry not being with her for their graduation prom? Olivia nodded and forced a smile.

"See you then. I've got to go." Grace took Doug's arm and headed for the dance floor.

The opening notes of Bobby Vinton's "Roses are Red" began. Longing slid through Olivia as she looked around the gymnasium one more time. Smiling graduates and their dates were moving onto the dance floor, leaving Olivia alone with her anxiety.

What could be keeping James? He'd said he would be late, but this was ridiculous. Should she call him? She'd never called his house. In all the months they'd been together, there'd never been a reason. James had always been available, attentive.

Unable to bear it any longer, Olivia skirted the tables and walked over to the entrance. The damp night air rushed toward her as she dashed down the steps.

Somewhere farther out in the parking lot she heard a car door slam. Away from the muted glare of the streetlights, a man started toward her, his loping stride so familiar. "James," she called. Heedless of her billowing skirt and the hours she'd spent arranging her hair, Olivia ran toward him.

She noticed his jeans and rumpled T-shirt first. The tense lines around James's eyes were visible, even in the uncertain light of the parking lot. "James, what is it?" she asked, holding out her arms.

He stopped just short of her reach. "Olivia," he said, his voice lacking its usual vigor, "there's…a problem. I can't stay here with you."

"Why? What's wrong?" She reached for his hand.

The stiff set of his shoulders warned her off. His eyes were dark, his jaw clenched as he shook his head. "Don't, Olivia. I have to go away. Please don't."

Shock reverberated through her. This couldn't be happening. James loved her.

Hot, sticky tears smudged her cheeks. "You were supposed to be here tonight. With me. This is *our* night, our time together. Tell me what's going on. I love you, James. You can't leave me."

Olivia swiped at her tears, fighting the urge to throw her arms around him. She had too much pride to force herself on James, and he clearly didn't want to touch her. "Did something happen to your dad?"

"I can't talk right now." He rubbed his dark sideburns with one hand, grimacing with pain.

"James, are you hurt?"

His glance edged past her. "I'm fine."

"No, you're not." Olivia moved closer. "What's wrong with your cheek? Is that a bruise?"

"Olivia, never mind about my face." He began to reach for her, then stopped. "Olivia, please understand I don't have a choice. My father knows about us."

"He knows about us? What do you mean? Hasn't he always?"

James rested his hands on his hips and his eyes studied the ground between them.

"You kept our relationship a secret?"

He nodded but didn't raise his eyes. "I knew my father wouldn't approve."

"James, look at me," she demanded.

He didn't meet her gaze.

"We're only weeks away from leaving for college, starting our life together. What has your father got to do with us?" She put out her hands but the flash of warning in his eyes forced them back to her sides.

"Olivia, I can't tell you very much, at least not yet. But things will be better soon. You have to trust me on this. You have to."

"I trust you. I always have, but I don't understand why you can't tell me what happened."

"My father wants me to go to Ireland," he said, "to the electronics plant there—"

"Ireland? Why Ireland?"

"He wants me to work for my Uncle Seamus. It won't be for long," he whispered, his Adam's apple straining against his throat as his gaze searched hers.

"What about college? Will you be back in time for college this fall?"

"I'll be back with you as soon as I can…. It'll all be over in a little while and we'll be together like we planned."

"But James, why can't we be together *now?* Tonight?"

"Olivia, this is such a mess, but I'll explain it all once I figure out what to do. You have to believe in us," he whispered, his eyes dark with misery. "You have to."

"Oh, James, I wanted tonight to be special." Unable to restrain herself any longer, she slid into his arms.

"I know you did. So did I. And I'll be back, trust me." He held her and the solid thudding of his heart allowed her to hope that everything was still okay between them. She clung to him, to his strength, breathing in his scent. Surely this was some sort of mistake.

He smoothed her hair from her face. "Olivia, I'm flying out in a few hours."

Tears burned her eyes again. "I'll go with you. I don't care where we are as long as we're together."

"You'll wait for me?" he asked, his expression bleak.

"Always," she whispered, hugging him to her.

His sudden intake of breath and a muffled moan startled her. "James, did I hurt you?"

He moved out of her embrace, his movements awkward and so unlike him. "I fell."

"When?"

"An hour or so ago. On the stairs. I hurt my ribs. It's not serious."

"Of course it's serious. Did you see a doctor? I'll go with you, if you want."

"Don't worry about it."

"Don't worry? You're injured, you're *leaving,* and I'm not supposed to worry?"

"Olivia, I have no choice but to be on that plane tonight—by myself."

Her heart beating painfully, Olivia made one last try to get him to tell her more. To explain why he had to go, what his father had said. "Look at me."

Olivia saw the self-loathing in his eyes and her heart rose in agony. "Whatever's wrong, we can fix it, you and I," she said urgently. "We have our whole lives ahead of us. If your father wants you to go to Ireland for a while, I'll go with you. We can come back later and go to college. You can't just walk away from me! We love each other. You'd never hurt me."

With a shuddering sigh, James turned and started back toward his car.

Tossing her pride, Olivia raced after him. "You can't leave me without telling me what went wrong! Why do you have to go?"

James turned back to face her, and anxiety clouded his once-adoring eyes. "I have no choice. I have to leave tonight."

"No!" Olivia wailed as she cast frantically about for some explanation. "Why? Doesn't your family approve of me? They've never even met me."

"Olivia, don't do this to yourself."

"Do what? Beg the man who loves me to stay with me?" Her voice shook. She stared at him, waiting for some sign that he might retract his horrifying words.

Silence.

Was he dumping her because he'd gotten what he wanted from her? Was she just a roll in the hay? After all, their families moved in different circles. His father the plant-owner, hers a laborer there. How… how Victorian. Regret lodged in the pit of her stomach. "I'm not good enough for you, is that it?"

"That's not true!" James half turned toward her.

"Then tell me the truth."

"I'll be back as soon as I can. That's all I can say right now."

Struggling to control the trembling in her hands, Olivia grabbed the gold chain around her neck and yanked it off, her skin burning in protest. James's class ring clattered across the cobblestones and rolled out of sight.

"There! Are you happy now? Take your ring and give it to some girl your father approves of. I'm sure he has someone in mind," she sobbed, tears streaming down her face.

"Olivia, please don't cry. Please don't. I have to go. If I don't, someone…might get hurt." James plowed his fingers through his hair, his gaze fixed on a point somewhere beyond her.

"What about *me?* What about how you're hurting me?"

He reached for her, then stopped, his hands suspended above her shoulders.

She held her breath, her whole body craving one last touch.

His fingers hovered over her, then came to rest at his sides. "I made a promise. Olivia, please don't hate me."

"I could never hate you. Oh, James, tell me what's wrong, okay? Whatever it is, we can work it out. That's what you always said—you and I, we can work anything out, because we love each other."

Had something destroyed his love for her? He

hadn't said he loved her, and James was always so quick to say it.

"Take me with you," she begged again.

"I can't," he said, before turning away a final time.

Struggling to find the right words, the words that would make James come back to her, Olivia followed him.

"I don't believe you could leave me like this. What about our future together, our plans?" she coaxed him, her heart a deadweight in her chest.

He didn't answer.

She watched him walk to his car and out of her life.

CHAPTER TWO

"MRS. MCELROY, you can see your husband now," the nurse said from the door of the room where Olivia sat. She hadn't moved since Dr. Crealock had talked to her, and she wasn't sure her legs would carry her. Taking a deep breath, she dared the words to leave her lips. "How's he doing?"

"He's still sedated, but you can continue to sit with him for brief periods," the nurse replied, leading Olivia back to his room, a room crowded with monitors, tubes and hundreds of things Olivia couldn't identify.

Beneath all the equipment, her husband lay on his back in the middle of the narrow bed. "James," she breathed as she made her way to his side.

"He won't be able to talk to you, but you can talk to him the same way you were doing before."

Olivia gently massaged his hand, feeling the leathery softness of his skin beneath her touch. His face had a pasty sheen, and his eyes were closed, just as they'd been when she was with him earlier. Alone in the strange room with its strange scents and sounds, she listened for the next breath from the man who held her very life in his hands.

"I'm here, darling. Your surgery is over. Now all you have to do is get better."

The room stood silent, except for the ping of a monitor and a whirring from a bottle on the wall. Outside a voice ordered Dr. Crealock to call admitting.

James's sudden intake of breath startled her. One of the huge machines gave a protesting beep. Olivia glanced first at James and then at the nursing station set amidst the glass-walled rooms. No one seemed to notice.

She grabbed a chair and pulled it close to the bed. With fear gnawing at the back of her throat, she rubbed his hand, willing him to wake up, to talk to her.

For what seemed like hours she sat waiting for James to open his eyes. But all she heard was the constant hum of equipment and the occasional urgent voice on the overhead paging system.

A nurse, her stethoscope draped around her neck, entered the room. "Mrs. McElroy, it's time for you to leave."

The nurse's kindly tone annoyed Olivia for some reason she couldn't identify. Maybe it was the fact that nothing Olivia said or did seemed to matter in this world of cool efficiency. Why couldn't they just let her stay here with James while she waited for him to wake up? "He doesn't seem to know I'm here. Are you sure he's not in a coma?"

The nurse checked the intravenous running into his left arm, her gaze never once meeting Olivia's. "He's medicated for the pain. He's doing as well as can be expected. Why don't you go to the coffee shop and get something to eat? It may be some time before Mr. McElroy can talk to you, and you need to keep your strength up."

She had no appetite and no interest in eating. She was afraid that if she left he might die while she was gone—an unreasonable fear, she supposed, but one that held her in its terrifying grip.

"I'd rather wait here." Olivia looked at James's face again, hoping to see some sign that he'd be with her soon. How could she manage without his strength? They'd had so little time together; there were so many things still unsaid…. "I'm worried. I'm so worried. My husband's never been sick like this."

The nurse touched her shoulder. "I understand how you must feel, but getting all worked up won't help. Why don't you take a break? We'll learn more when Dr. Crealock comes back."

"When will that be?"

"In an hour or two."

"I'm trying to reach my son to tell him what's happened. I'd like to speak to Dr. Crealock when he's back. Would you let him know?"

"Certainly, but in the meantime…"

The look on the nurse's face told Olivia that her presence was delaying nursing procedures that needed to be done. Holding back all the pleading words, all the arguments as to why she should stay, Olivia rose from the chair. "I'll be in the waiting room."

OLIVIA STEADIED the cell phone in her trembling hands as she called Kyle's office in Geneva. After years of teaching anthropology at Western Michigan University, Kyle had dropped everything to go to work in Switzerland for a ski lift company, of all things.

Olivia knew little about Kyle's life since he'd walked out and she still didn't understand why he'd quit his teaching job.

Kyle hadn't returned her call when she'd tried before, so she'd left an urgent message, asking him to call her without saying what was wrong. Deep down, she feared that he'd simply ignore any message concerning James, and it pained her to think her son could be so unforgiving.

She wanted to hear Kyle's voice, to be reassured that he cared. The phone had rung for the fifth time when she finally heard a woman's voice. Olivia asked for Kyle.

"He's not here."

"When do you expect him?"

"He didn't say." The disinterest in the girl's voice didn't bode well for any success in finding her son.

"Listen, it's his mother. I left an urgent message for Kyle, and he didn't call me back. I need to reach him as soon as possible."

"Kyle's not here, and I can't reach him. He may have got his messages off his voice mail. I have no way of knowing."

Why would Kyle hire anyone as lackluster as this woman? "Do you expect to hear from him today?" she asked, not trying to hide her impatience.

"He usually checks in with us at some point. I'll tell him to call you."

The conversation was going nowhere, while valuable time was being lost. Even if this lethargic-sounding girl got the message to Kyle, it would be at least twelve hours before he could get out of Geneva and back to Boston.

Anything could happen in that time.

"Please tell Kyle it's very important that he call me on my cell phone, day or night." She gave the girl her number again and hung up.

She was about to visit the coffee shop the nurse

had mentioned when Dr. Crealock appeared at the door of the waiting room.

"Mrs. McElroy, you wanted to talk to me?"

Her heart overwhelmed by dread, she followed his every movement as he entered the room and sat in the chair beside her. "Yes, I did. Has anything changed? Is James going to wake up soon?"

"Mrs. McElroy, please be patient. I've ordered a full body scan to look for any damage. We're doing everything possible to ensure that he recovers. All his vital signs are stable, and his heart is working fine, despite the extensive surgery to repair the valve and replace the coronary arteries."

If James was with her, he'd be asking all kinds of questions, wanting an explanation of the clotting problem and the surgery. But Olivia didn't dare ask. She couldn't bring herself to consider the danger her husband faced if a clot blocked a critical part of his body.

If James was with her, he'd smile and tell her to look on the bright side. She'd endure anything to see her husband smile again.

Tears simmered against her eyelids as memories rushed through her. She wished with all her heart that things had turned out differently. That circumstances had not betrayed them…

"OLIVIA, wait for me," Grace called as she raced down the steps of Harrison's Drugstore. "Where are you going in such a hurry?"

Grace's carefree attitude, once so appealing, now grated on Olivia's nerves. Olivia hadn't known a carefree moment since James had left for Ireland. She'd spent every waking hour after that trying to figure out what had driven him away from her. "I have to get home."

Olivia couldn't look at her friend after what had happened at the prom. James had left without a word of explanation, and Olivia had been put in the awkward position of making excuses why he hadn't shown up. That was the first of many lies she'd been forced to tell.

She'd tried to reach him, but the housekeeper refused to take a message. After weeks of sleepless nights and of feeling increasingly ill, her parents had insisted she see their family doctor….

"I have Dad's car," Grace cajoled. "Let me drive you. *Please* tell me what's going on. Why won't you talk to me?"

As much as she loved her friend, Olivia didn't want to be around Grace at the moment. "No, I'll walk. I need the exercise." The excuse slipped out so easily.

Grace grabbed her arm. "What's wrong with you? You didn't show up at Bennie's after the prom.

You haven't returned any of my calls since then. I went by the other night, and your mother said you weren't feeling well. Tell me what's the matter," Grace insisted, frustration showing in her eyes.

Olivia wanted to throw her arms around her friend and sob out her story, to have Grace offer sympathy and understanding when she confided how her life had changed forever. But shame held her back. "Nothing. I'm fine."

"I thought you trusted me."

"I can't talk right now."

"So when *can* you talk?"

Olivia met Grace's anxious gaze, aware that in a few days she probably wouldn't see Grace again for a very long time. But confiding in Grace would cause anguish and embarrassment to those she loved most in this world. "I don't know," she said.

Grace's blue shorts fit her slim body perfectly, and her matching blue top showed too much cleavage in Olivia's opinion. But Olivia recognized that these were jealous thoughts. Her own days of prancing around in short shorts were over.

But even more than that, it saddened her to know that she would leave her home and her friends with a lie on her lips and the betrayal of someone she loved in her heart.

Her parents had been upset and anxious enough when she'd told them James had gone to Ireland, but when she revealed that she was pregnant… She'd never forget the shock and grief in their eyes.

Determined to save face, her parents had spent hours searching for the best place she could live while she waited for her baby to be born, somewhere out of town and away from their friends and the curious, condemning looks of their neighbors.

"I'm leaving town tomorrow."

"You're going to Hastings this early?" Grace raised her eyebrows in question.

Olivia had had to notify Hastings College that she wouldn't be attending in the fall, and it had been the hardest call she'd ever made. "No, I'm going into nurse's training in Bangor."

It was the lie she'd agreed to tell when people asked. Bangor was too far away for anyone to check, and by the time they did, she'd actually be living in Bar Harbor with her aunt and uncle.

"Nurse's training? Why?"

The genuine concern in Grace's eyes made Olivia feel so lonely, but she'd promised her parents that she wouldn't tell anyone. And she would keep that promise. It was the only way she could do right by her family. "It's what I want."

"What you want? I don't believe you, Olivia. I know how much you wanted to go to Hastings, how many plans you and James had."

Olivia fought back the urge to say what was in her heart. "Things change."

Tears ran unhindered down Grace's cheeks as she slipped one hand into the pocket of her shorts. "I guess they do. I hear that James is in Ireland and isn't coming back anytime soon. Knowing how bad you must feel, I wanted to help you, but if this is how it's going to be…" She gave a hopeless shrug. "I brought you something." She held out James's class ring. "This was on the ground in the school parking lot. I don't know how it got there, but I do know it's yours." She passed the ring to Olivia.

Olivia stared at the ring, at the inscription inside the band—a swirling script of the words *Love is Eternal.* Struggling to control her despair, Olivia wrapped her arms around her friend. "Thank you so much. You have no idea what this means to me. I'll never forget you, Grace."

Grace hugged her back. "You'd better not."

"And I promise I'll call you just as soon as I can."

"Double promise?" Grace smiled, wiping away her tears.

"Double promise." Clutching James's ring to her heart, Olivia watched her friend leave. A strange heaviness engulfed her as she started the long walk back to her house. She would never understand how James could abandon her to a life in Bar Harbor without him.

HALF AN HOUR later, she reached the safety of her back door, thankful that for a little while she could be free of prying questions.

Everyone wanted to know why someone as smart as Olivia Banks wasn't going to college. Why she and James had broken up. She had no answers.

"Oh, honey, is that you?" her mother asked, holding the phone out to Olivia as she entered the narrow hall from the kitchen. "It's for you," she said.

"Who is it?"

Placing her hand over the receiver, her mother whispered, "I don't recognize the voice, but she sounds anxious." She gave Olivia the faintest of smiles. "I'll be in the kitchen when you're done."

Olivia slid onto the tiny needlepoint-covered chair beside the hall table. "Hello."

"Hi, Olivia. This is Julia, James's sister."

"Is James home? Is he all right?" she asked, hope charging through her.

"No, he's in Ireland. He called here last night, and I took the call. He told me he left you in a big rush, and he said to say how sorry he was."

"What else did he say?"

"Not much, except he's lonely, and so am I. Things are such a mess around here. Dad doesn't speak to me, and if he discovers I talked to James, there'll be trouble."

Olivia wanted to offer consoling words, words

that would ease Julia's discomfort, but all she could think about was the fact that she was alone without any way of contacting James, of telling him about the baby. "Do you have a phone number where I can reach him?"

"No, and Dad's forbidden me to talk to him. My own brother! I didn't know Dad could be so mean, but I hope he'll get over this, and let James come back before college starts in the fall."

"I don't get it. Why is your father so upset? Why did James have to go to Ireland?"

"James went because if he didn't, I would've been sent to a strict private boarding school. James knew I didn't want that."

"Why would your father send you away?"

"Because I helped James keep his relationship with you a secret, that's why. As it is, I'm grounded for the next month, and it could be longer, if Dad thinks I'm talking to my brother— or you. But Olivia there's something I have to tell you, something James wanted you to know. He asked me to call you for him."

Everything was going to be all right. James would come back for her. Olivia held her breath, waiting for his words of love. "Tell me."

"James wanted to warn you not to let your parents talk to Dad about you and him. If they do, my father will fire your father and call in the loan the company has on your house. And my father would do it, I know he would. With Dad against your parents, there wouldn't be a bank willing to lend them money. Your parents would lose their home."

Olivia muffled a cry of distress. "Your father can't do that! Why would he want to hurt my dad that way? He's always been a good worker, so loyal."

"My father doesn't want your family meddling in what he sees as family business. I know that because I was listening at the door when I heard him yell at James."

"Yelling at James? *Why?*"

"Olivia I can't talk any longer. I have to go. If anyone tells my father I called you—"

"Please, just give me a minute." There was no point in trying to pass on a message to James if Julia was so afraid of her father. Olivia remembered how James had pulled away from her in those last moments they'd spent together. "Julia," she asked abruptly, "did James fall?"

"Fall? No, why do you ask?"

"The night he left James said he'd fallen and hurt his ribs."

"I doubt that. I'm sure he would've told me…."

Olivia heard someone yelling in the background. "I have to go, but don't forget what I said," Julia whispered.

"I won't." Olivia hung up the phone, her

thoughts moving from James to Julia and the threat her parents faced. Trying to remain calm, she made her way to the kitchen. "Mom, can I help you get supper?"

"Who was that on the phone?" Her mother's expression was one Olivia had come to recognize, suspicion mixed with anxiety.

"Just a friend." She wouldn't tell her what Julia had said, not unless she had to. Knowing that the man her father had worked for all his life could be so cruel, so vindictive, would only add to her parents' anxiety.

Her father and mother had been elated about the possibility that she and James would marry after they graduated from college. Her mother had talked of nothing else in the weeks leading up to the prom. Excited talk about how they'd be making wedding plans someday. How much they wanted to be grandparents.

Despite their disappointment in the past weeks, her parents had pitched in and arranged for her to go and live in Bar Harbor with her dad's sister. She'd be on the bus tomorrow heading out of town and away from all the trouble she'd caused.

"Come with me for a minute," her mother said, obviously on edge. Her lips were pursed, her shoulders stiff and straight.

Olivia followed her mother to the den, her

thoughts on how much more she had to do before she boarded the bus in the morning.

"Sit down." Her mother nodded to a chair by the window that looked out onto the vegetable garden so carefully tended by her father.

"What is it, Mom?"

"Your father and I have talked it over. We feel you should give the baby up for adoption."

Shock slammed into Olivia's heart. "Give up my baby? I can't—"

"I know you have a lot on your mind at the moment, but you have to realize that you can't support a child."

"I'll get a job, and I'll save money. Mom, I *can't* give my baby away. I can't."

"Olivia, without any money from the father of your child, how do you expect to raise it? Lord knows your dad and I can't afford to keep you *and* a baby."

Olivia stared at her mother. The hope that James would come back and claim her and their unborn child was all that kept her from falling apart.

She could not believe that James didn't want her. James had been forced to go to Ireland to work in the family business there, but surely it wouldn't be for long. He'd always said his parents expected him to get a college education. They'd relent and let him come home when college started in the fall. And when he came back, he'd want her and their baby with him.

In the meantime, she'd go to her aunt's house and wait for their baby to be born. "Mom, things will work out, you'll see."

"No, Olivia, it's time to face reality. Things are *not* going to work out, or that poor excuse for a man would be here with you. If James won't marry you, and if you won't agree to adoption, your father and I plan to contact his father. Mr. McElroy can well afford—"

"Don't, Mom! Please don't do that."

"Olivia, be reasonable. You're pregnant by a man who doesn't have the guts to step forward and take responsibility. Now you want your mother and father to foot the bill while you wait for him to come back. And there's no guarantee of *that*."

Her mother's voice was loud and threatening. For the first time since she'd learned she was pregnant, Olivia was truly scared. "That's not how it is at all. I just need a chance to sort everything out. I can't decide about adoption right this minute. It wouldn't be fair to my baby or to me."

"And what about us—your parents? What's fair for us? You announce you're pregnant, and that the father's run off to Ireland without a word of explanation. Meanwhile, you fantasize that he'll come back to you. Olivia, you've got to accept the facts. You're on your own with no husband to support you. The father of your child abandoned you. Now you're the one who's going through the shame and embarrassment of being an unwed mother with no prospects."

Olivia listened with dread, knowing what her mother would do. She'd march right up to the plant offices and demand that James be brought back from Ireland.

Olivia would rather be alone for the rest of her life than face the humiliation of being rejected once again by the man who'd deserted her, leaving her to cope with the aftermath of that night at the prom. If James wanted her—and she believed he did—he'd be back for her. If not, there was nothing she was prepared to do.

"One last time, Olivia. James is the father, and he has to take responsibility," her mother warned, her lips tight with anger.

If it would keep her mother from going to James's family, she'd tell her what he'd said. "Mom, you and Dad have a loan on this house through the company, don't you?"

"What do you know about it?"

"If you try to interfere, his father will call in the loan. And Dad will lose his job."

The air hissed through her mother's lips. "Olivia, Tom McElroy wouldn't do any such thing. Your father's a good worker. His supervisor at the plant said as much."

"It's not about Dad, or the fact that he's a good worker. It's about us staying out of James's life."

Her mother's anguished expression would live in her memory, a reminder of the grief she'd brought her parents.

"But how will you manage if you don't get financial help from his family? If you're going to keep this baby, you have to have money."

Fear wrapped its cold tentacles around Olivia's heart. "I'm going to do what's right for my baby. I'll get a job, and I'll save money."

"Yes, until your employer tells you he can't have a pregnant woman on the premises, and then what will you do?"

Humiliation burned deep. "Surely you and Dad could lend me some money for a few months. I'll pay you back."

"We're willing to provide you with as much money as we can afford, but not if you refuse to put the child up for adoption."

Desperation threatened to destroy all the defenses Olivia had so carefully put in place when James walked away. What would she do alone, without her parents' support? "You refuse to help me unless I agree to give up my baby?"

"That's the reality, Olivia. We don't have the

money to support you and your baby in Bar Harbor, and you can't come back here without a father for your baby. What else do you expect us to do?" Her mother's eyes were dark with righteous indignation.

"Mom, you don't mean it. You can't."

"Olivia, we love you, and we want the best for you. But raising a child on your own is not what's best. Have the baby and let someone adopt it. Remember, if you keep the baby, no man worth anything will want to marry you and provide for some other man's child. Keeping the baby means you can forget all about going to college. Your scholarship to Hastings was the chance of a lifetime. Please think about what you're doing. Imagine what your life will be like with no husband to pay the bills. You'll have to leave your child with a sitter and go out to work. And without an education…"

Olivia had thought of little else in the past weeks. But giving up her baby to be raised by strangers was something she just couldn't do.

CHAPTER THREE

SIX WEEKS LATER, Olivia smiled as she made change for one of the regulars at Crawford's Steak House. Bar Harbor's top restaurant had been busy all evening, the kind of busy that kept Olivia's loneliness at bay.

She'd cried all the way to Bar Harbor, tears that made her feel even lonelier. But tears wouldn't solve her need for money when her baby arrived.

She missed her mother's caring and attention, but they'd parted on such bad terms she held out no hope that they could ever be close again. And it crushed Olivia to think her mother could be so cruel.

She'd called home a couple of times, but the conversations were distant and awkward. On her eighteenth birthday, her parents had sent her a check in the mail.

During those last days in their house, Olivia hadn't heard a word from James. Still, every night she'd dreamed of him. The dream was always so sweet, so full of love and hope, she wanted to stay asleep forever. Every morning she awoke to the bitter truth. James had abandoned her and their baby.

She'd never experienced such fear as she did when she climbed off the bus in Bar Harbor to be met by a stern-faced aunt and uncle who wanted her to account for her every waking moment.

And with no one to confide in, Olivia felt completely isolated and alone.

Yet the thought of the baby growing inside her made life bearable. With each passing day, she grew to love her child and tried to imagine what he or she would look like. Would the baby's eyes be dark like hers or blue like James's? She spent hours fantasizing about life with her child. Boy or girl, it didn't matter to her. She pictured reading to the baby, walking along the beach with her toddler…

Luck had been with her when she started looking for work. Crawford's had advertised for a hostess, and not daring to reveal her secret, she'd answered the ad. To her complete surprise, she'd gotten the job.

It was the evening shift, but that was a lucky break as well. She was too sick in the mornings to lift her head off the pillow. Her aunt had taken pity on her and stayed with her through the frightening bouts of morning sickness, but her kindness couldn't disguise the disappointment Olivia saw in her eyes.

Each day Olivia watched everyone who entered the restaurant and waited for James to come and rescue her. And as the days dragged by she told herself to be patient. He'd asked her to wait for him, and she would. He didn't know she was pregnant, but she had to believe that when he found out, he'd want their baby as much as she did. Each day, she asked her aunt if there was mail for her, and each day the answer was the same.

Olivia couldn't confide in anyone at work because she was afraid that her boss, Alex Crawford, would learn about her baby and fire her. In the meantime, she was working every shift she could get and saving her money.

Ever so gradually, she was beginning to make the adjustment to being on her own. Still, as the evening shift came to an end, the thought of going back to her aunt and uncle's house was depressing. Their distrusting behavior heightened Olivia's insecurity.

"Ready to close up?" Alex Crawford asked as he came out of the office behind the bar.

She glanced at him and caught his smile. Doris, one of the waitresses, had told her that Alex was thirty-two, but he didn't seem that old to her. With his smile and charm, he reminded her of Grace's older brother, Nathan.

Alex was a hard worker and easy to get along

with, but this was the first time he'd been in his office during the evening. He was usually gone shortly after she came in for her shift.

"Yeah, I'm ready to go. It's been a long night, but a good one. We had the entire fire department in here earlier, and they were a lot of fun."

Alex chuckled. "Glad to hear they behaved themselves." He strolled around the restaurant, surveying the area while he straightened an arrangement of potted plants near the back. Returning to stand beside her at the cash register, he watched as she cashed out for the night. Because it was her turn to do the night deposit, she was the only staff member in the restaurant.

"Would you like to have a cup of coffee with me? I want to talk to you about something."

Olivia shrugged. She'd be fired if anyone knew she was pregnant. In an upscale restaurant like Crawford's, obviously pregnant women didn't deal with the public. "Sure," she said, her thoughts racing.

What would she do if he fired her? Where would she find the money to live on? She couldn't stay with her aunt and uncle past the baby's birth, nor did she want to. She followed Alex to a booth in the corner, sliding in across from him.

"Olivia, you've been doing a great job here at the restaurant for nearly two months now," he began, "and I want to thank you for all your hard work."

Here it comes, she thought to herself, wishing she hadn't splurged on new shoes to ease the cramps in her legs caused by being on her feet all the time.

"You're welcome. I really enjoy working here. The patrons are great and the work's actually kind of fun," she said, recognizing the truth of her words as she said them. She liked the restaurant business. She liked the hustle and enjoyed pleasing their customers. She also liked the staff—and especially Alex.

Alex clasped his hands on the table between them and looked her straight in the eye. "Olivia, I'd like you to take over as manager here. I have other business interests that require my attention. I can rely on you to do what needs to be done here."

She gasped. "But…I don't have any business experience. I'm too young. I wouldn't know how to manage. I'm sure there are other people who'd do a better job. I appreciate the offer, but—"

"No 'buts' about it. I've tried in the past to get some of the staff to take over, but they don't want the responsibility. And with so many people headed for jobs in Boston or Portland, it's hard to find good employees."

He gave her an assessing stare, and continued before she could respond. "Olivia, you've done a great job as hostess and cashier on the evening shift. The previous evening hostess was constantly calling me with problems, while you just took right over and did the job. I can teach you every-thing you'd need to know and help you adjust to your new responsibilities. I'm sure you'll learn fast. Above all, I want you here."

His words lifted her spirits and she laughed out loud. "Thank you."

He ducked his head as he smiled at her, a boyish look on his face. "Is that a yes?"

Alex was offering her a fulltime job, meaning she'd have the money to look after herself until she had to leave. But how could she accept the position when she'd be forced to resign in a few months? She'd disappoint Alex, and she almost certainly wouldn't get a job offer like this again. Would he have made this offer if he'd been aware that she was pregnant? Should she tell him now? And risk losing this chance?

She had to think of her child, and what she'd do about work after the baby was born. Being the manager at Crawford's pretty much guaranteed her a job at any restaurant in town when she was ready to resume work as a new mother. Could she really refuse such a good offer?

"It's a yes, and thank you so much," she answered, returning his smile.

Alex took her hands in his. "I'm the one who should be thanking you. Why don't we celebrate? We could give the competition a little business, or we could stay right here. This may surprise you, but I know my way around the kitchen."

His gaze locked with hers, and in a flash of insight, Olivia wondered if he had more than business on his mind.

But in the end, she had nothing to worry about. Alex had taken her out to dinner at a quiet inn a few miles outside town and behaved like a perfect gentleman. Olivia enjoyed having a man pay attention to her.

Once she started her new job as evening manager, dinner together once a week became a pleasant habit, and Olivia had started to look forward to their evenings together. Alex always had advice for her when she needed his help with her new job, always listened to her and gave her every indication that they were friends.

While lingering over coffee at a nearby diner one night, talking business, Alex leaned across the table. "You're different from most women I've known."

A tiny warning sounded in Olivia. "What do you mean?"

"You're so…genuine, so compassionate with people. The staff all like you, the patrons seek you out, and even Harry, my perpetually unhappy chef, likes you. On top of that, you're easy to talk to."

Olivia could feel her cheeks glow under the barrage of compliments. "That's so kind of you. I love the restaurant business. And I want to be a success at my job."

"What else do you want, Olivia?" Alex's intense scrutiny forced Olivia to look away. What she wanted would forever be her secret.

An uncomfortable silence followed while Olivia tried to come up with an answer to his question, one that wouldn't reveal too much about her past. She wanted Alex to like her, but not if it involved sharing her personal history. Everything she did from now on was for her baby, including her job. "I want to be happy, to be accepted, to have someone care about me."

Alex's shoulders lifted. He rubbed his jaw, his voice hesitant. "I can relate to that. Have you ever done something you're ashamed of? Something you'd do anything to make right again?"

Did Alex know about her situation? Instinctively, she eased away from him. "I guess so. Haven't we all?"

Alex played with his napkin. "I was married several years ago, and my wife died giving birth to our son."

Doris had told Olivia about Alex's wife, and

Olivia felt a deep sympathy for him. Despite everything she'd been through, losing her unborn child was unthinkable. "I'm so sorry. I can only imagine what it must've been like."

His eyes were sincere as he searched her face. "It was awful, and I acted like a complete jerk," he said. "I made a bad mistake, one I'll always regret."

The plea in his voice told her he needed to confide in her. Was she prepared to have him tell her something that would lead to greater closeness between them?

Alex had always been kind and fair to her. Being friends with him meant a lot, and if she could offer some comfort... "I know all about making mistakes," she murmured.

Alex leaned back. "Not like this. I was a selfish fool when I married Anna. My parents covered for me, no matter what kind of trouble I got into. I guess they thought they were showing their love for me, but it was the worst thing they could've done. I was a headstrong teenager with too much money and a fast car."

"Sometimes parents don't see the damage they've done until it's too late," she said.

"We got married a week after my twentieth birthday. I wasn't much of a husband. Anna got pregnant a couple of years later, and I didn't have enough common sense to see she needed me.

Even if I had, I probably wouldn't have had the maturity to help her."

"What happened?" she asked, surprised at the pain in his voice.

"Anna went into labor while I was away at a stock car race. Mom called me to come home, but I knew it all, so I waited until the racing day was over, and drove back that night. When I arrived at the hospital, my wife and son were dead."

Olivia couldn't believe her ears. The Alex she knew would never do such a thing. Olivia saw the raw truth in his expression, his need for comfort—and confession. "It must have been terrible," she said, touching his hand.

Relief shone from his eyes as he tucked her hand in his. "You're the only person I've ever told. I let everyone think I'd simply been too late. If my friends had known that I'd intentionally not come home when Anna went into labor, they would've disowned me. I couldn't face that. And as for my parents…" He shrugged.

"But it's over now, and there's nothing you can do to change the past."

"That's the whole problem. There *is* nothing I can do, no way I can make up for my mistake. I wasn't there when my son was born, or when he and Anna lost their lives."

Alex shifted in his seat, his gaze locked on her. "I'd give anything to make amends to Anna, to my son. Anything at all."

The remorse on Alex's face and the tears in his eyes were her undoing. James wouldn't be there for the birth of his child, and she knew nothing could change that, either.

Tears rose and spilled down her cheeks. Afraid of losing control, Olivia swiped at them.

"What's wrong? Oh hell, I didn't mean to make you cry." Scrambling out of the booth and coming around to her side, Alex slid in beside her.

Feeling a profound sense of loss, needing to be comforted herself, she succumbed to the warmth of his arms and snuggled against his chest.

Desperate for someone to confide in, Olivia sobbed out her own story—about losing James, about being pregnant, how afraid she felt. Alex didn't flinch, nor did he turn away. And when her tears stopped, he raised her chin and smiled at her. "I wish I could've been there for you."

If only she'd had a brother like Alex… "Me, too."

"You're a very brave woman, Olivia, and I'm glad we're friends."

Brave? She'd never thought of herself that way, and his words eased all the hurt and longing she'd carried with her over the past four months. "You mean it?" she asked.

He nodded and smiled.

That was when the tension began to slide away.

AFTER THAT NIGHT, Alex joined Olivia when she closed the restaurant every evening and they had dinner together while they talked about business, and about their lives. She'd grown to appreciate Alex's steadiness, and the kindness he showed his staff. One of his nicest qualities was the respect he consistently showed her. And he seldom missed an opportunity to talk to her, making her feel special.

Whenever he came into the restaurant, they'd go into the office and discuss any outstanding problems. He made a point of telling her where he'd be if she needed him for anything, his tender glance implying that should she need him for anything *personal,* he'd be available for that, too. He could usually be reached at one of the three Ford dealerships he owned in the Portland and Bar Harbor areas.

Never once did he mention her pregnancy, and she was pretty sure he hadn't told anyone. But very soon, people would see the changes in her body and begin asking questions. Then her days of working at Crawford's would have to end. Alex hadn't said a word to that effect, but it was common sense.

When he'd arrived this particular evening for their usual dinner, he hovered near the cash. Once things had finally quieted down and the dinner guests and staff were gone, he turned to her. "Olivia, I can't tell you how much better this restaurant is operating with you in charge."

"Thank you. I love flattery," she said, glancing up from her work. She had all the money sorted and ready for deposit on the way home.

"It's not flattery." His tone softened as his strong hands stilled hers. "Olivia, I've discovered something over the past few months."

"Discovered—what?"

"I've come to realize just how much your friendship means to me. It always brightens my day to walk in here and see you in charge, working with such enthusiasm." He paused. "After you make the deposit tonight, I want to take you out somewhere special to celebrate your success."

"That sounds nice, but it's not necessary. I like my job and—"

"Remember," he broke in, "I'm the one who said you could do it. It's my celebration, too."

How could she argue? And besides, she needed to get away from the cool reproach she faced every night at her aunt and uncle's.

They chose a secluded booth at Dillon's—their

chief competitor—just a few blocks from the waterfront, where they ordered a late dinner. The seafood casserole tasted delicious and the wine Alex selected was redolent of peaches and warm summer afternoons. "What a wonderful meal," she said, moving her empty plate aside before meeting his watchful gaze.

"And more to come, I hope," he said, a slight smile on his face. "You remember the night we confided in each other?"

How could she forget? "Yes."

"I've never been able to talk to anyone like that, ever. After that night I began to see how lonely my life had become. You've made a difference to me," he said, a hint of shyness in his voice.

Alex Crawford shy? Olivia wondered. "I consider you my friend, someone who was there for me when I needed support," she said, and only then did she realize how much she relied on his friendship. She shuddered at the thought of what her life in Bar Harbor would've been like if he hadn't taken an interest in her.

Alex took her hand. "Ever since I met you, I've felt this connection, this feeling that you and I belong together. Haven't you?"

She shied away from the eagerness in his eyes, a look that said he wanted more from her than friendship. But she didn't need anything more, and she owed it to him to make that clear. "Alex, I haven't had the time or energy to think of anything other than my work." And my baby, she thought but didn't say.

"Olivia, you must've noticed that I've spent a lot more time at the restaurant than I need to and it's because of you. When I'm away, I miss your smile, the way you make me feel special when I walk in the door. I love the way you seem to know when I've had a rough day, or when I need to talk about something besides work. I don't spend much time with my friends anymore. It's all because of you, and how much I need you in my life."

She didn't know what to say, how to respond. "Alex, I like you, too, and I enjoy your company. We make a good team."

"Yes, we are a good team and together we can do anything. I've given what I'm about to say a great deal of thought."

The determination in Alex's eyes made Olivia want to move away from him, but she resisted the urge. Alex wouldn't do anything to intentionally make her feel uncomfortable. She trusted him. "You've given what a great deal of thought?" she asked.

"You and me. I want us to be closer, not just friends."

Somehow, Olivia had suspected this moment was coming, and she was suddenly afraid. "But…you don't know me."

"I know all I need to know. I want to be with you, every day and night. Olivia, will you marry me?"

His words made it impossible to breathe. Marry him? How could she marry anyone but James? "I…I'm not sure what to say. No, I can't. It's too…sudden."

He slid his chair closer to hers. "I understand it's sudden, and that I took you by surprise, but it doesn't change how I feel. I've waited for someone like you. I didn't plan to propose like this. I had every intention of saying these words over champagne and roses on the deck of a cruise ship, but I couldn't wait."

Olivia's breath burned her throat. The last thing she'd expected from Alex was a marriage proposal. She didn't love him, and he hadn't said he loved her. But she *did* like him.

And besides, her experience with love didn't have much to recommend it. Alex was kind and generous, and he'd protect her and her unborn child from gossip when her child was born.

How she wished she could talk to her mother and father right now, to ask them what she should do. They'd be happy that she had a chance at a respectable marriage and a new life with a father for her child. Loneliness, like a blast of chilled air, made her shiver.

In her heart of hearts, she wanted James to be with her when their baby was born. It wasn't going to happen and that pained her more than she'd thought possible. She loved James, she always would. But he was gone from her life without a trace, without a word of explanation. He hadn't come back to go to college, and he hadn't been in contact with her since he'd left.

Yet, despite everything, she'd clung to the belief that he'd return for her. But maybe her mother was right. Maybe it was time she faced reality rather than continue this dream.

"Alex, you're such a sweet man, but have you thought this through? You'd be marrying a woman who'll give birth to another's man's child. How would you feel about that?"

"I'd be proud to become a father, to finally do something good for someone else. My whole life's been selfish and shallow. Talking about all of this with you has made me understand myself better."

His touch was gentle as he tilted up her chin. "Let's put the past in the past and start now. New beginnings for both of us. What do you say? Will you marry me?"

Over the past months, Olivia had come to love her unborn child, a love that consumed her. There was no way in the world that she could put her baby up for adoption. Having Alex as her husband would end her worries about keeping the child. If he provided her baby with a good home, she would do her best to make Alex happy. She glanced at the nervous smile on his face, and her heart warmed.

Alex and she were friends, and that was the best place to start building a relationship. Love would come later. This was her one big chance to make a positive change in her life. What did she have to lose? "Yes, I'll marry you."

He sighed and followed it with an anxious laugh. "That was easy, wasn't it?"

He reached into the inside pocket of his sport jacket and brought out a jeweler's box, snapping the lid open. A large square-cut diamond twinkled in the candlelight. "I hope you like it."

He took her hand in his and slid the ornate ring on her finger. The kiss immediately afterward was gentle and searching. But Olivia had hardly adjusted to his lips on hers before he intensified it and pressed his body to hers.

Olivia yielded to the demands of his mouth while she tried to stop comparing Alex's kiss to James's. It wasn't fair to Alex, but Olivia couldn't halt the memories of James's mouth on hers, and the heat that rushed through her body at his touch.

Sensing her lack of enthusiasm, Alex pulled away. "Olivia, darling, I know this is all a shock, but I'm going to make you happy. I promise," he said, running his fingers along her cheek.

Olivia didn't have to wait very long to find out. They were married with his best friends, Earle and Linda Shay, as witnesses. And Olivia moved into his mother's towering Gothic mansion overlooking the harbor while they waited for their new home to be built.

Her parents and her aunt and uncle attended the wedding, clearly pleased that she'd made a decision they could approve.

She'd actually seen her mother smile during the wedding reception—but not at her.

IF ONLY SHE'D known then what she knew now, life would've been very different. She glanced around the far-too-familiar waiting room, her fingers tapping on the armrests. Dr. Crealock hadn't put her mind at ease one tiny bit, and still no word from Kyle. The nurse hadn't returned to tell her she could go back into James's room, and in her rush to follow the ambulance, she hadn't thought about what she might need while she waited.

Restless, she got up from the chair and went to the window that faced the roof of an adjoining building. The muffled hum of a busy hospital was broken by the one voice Olivia dreaded to hear.

"Did anyone think to call me?" Susan McElroy demanded as her dour-faced attendant wheeled her into the room.

Olivia turned. "I left a message on your voice mail."

"Am I supposed to thank you for that?" the older woman asked.

"It's up to you," Olivia said, making the decision to leave the waiting room at the earliest possible moment. There were few people in the world Olivia could honestly say she hated, but Susan McElroy was one of them.

Head up and shoulders back, she rolled past Olivia, her drooping chest festooned with a large gold cross hanging from a filigreed gold chain. "I've been told my son is doing as well as can be expected, whatever the hell that means."

"Your son has developed a complication, something to do with clotting." Olivia rubbed the knot of tension building in her neck.

Susan dug her fingers into the arms of the wheelchair, her face turning a pale, sickly color. "What do you mean, a complication? Not a blood clot, surely?"

"Is there a history of clotting in the family?"

"Yes, there is. Should I talk to the doctors?" Olivia noted that Susan looked every one of her eighty-five years as she tried to steady her shaking hands in her lap. "I don't want to lose my son. Not my son."

Olivia didn't want to talk about James with Susan McElroy. The woman had lost any right to be part of her son's life long ago.

"Mrs. McElroy, I think the doctors would appreciate any information you could give them. And I'm sorry about your son. I understand how it feels to worry about a child."

Her head bent, Susan clawed frantically at the gold cross.

"I realize this is difficult for you," Olivia offered halfheartedly.

Susan stared up into her face, eyes shining with tears. "Well, I guess I should be thankful that you were with him when it happened. Ever since his bout with rheumatic fever as a child, James has been very stubborn when it comes to getting medical help for himself."

Olivia had often hoped that this woman, who had denied her existence all these years, would come to accept her. And now, as she watched Susan, Olivia knew just how little it mattered to her what the woman thought. "I only want what's best for James."

"Well, at least we can agree on that. I'm going

to talk to the doctor," Susan said, signaling her attendant to wheel her from the room.

Knowing how much Susan McElroy liked to be in charge, Olivia assumed that Dr. Crealock was about to be confronted by someone who'd insist on sharing her views of the medical community in general and him in particular. Then she'd give him his orders with the stern approach of an army commander. Olivia hoped Dr. Crealock was ready to defend any action he took in relation to James.

AN HOUR LATER, Olivia entered the coffee shop on the main level. Hospital staff, wearing uniforms in all colors of the rainbow, stood in line at the checkout, or sat in groups, their conversation punctuated by the urgent bleat of pagers.

Olivia perused the selection of doughnuts, cookies and squares, searching for something that appealed to her. Nothing did, but to keep the staff from lecturing her, she chose a cookie and picked up a coffee. A short elevator ride brought her back to the waiting area outside Intensive Care, where she settled in to wait for her next chance to see James.

His mother hadn't returned to the waiting area, which probably meant that, as usual, she'd gotten her way and had talked to the doctor. Olivia could easily imagine the battle she'd pitched to get into James's room.

Thinking about James brought back the now-familiar lump in her throat. She had to believe that this crisis would be over soon, and they'd go back to their life together. Then they could try again to make amends to Kyle. There had to be a way to bring Kyle into their lives.

She dialed her son's number one more time, but got his voice mail again. Damn! What could he be doing that would keep him away from the phone this long? She didn't want to think of the alternative—that he was intentionally not calling her.

A rustling sound in the corridor made Olivia glance toward the door. Olivia braced for yet another unpleasant encounter with Susan McElroy.

Instead Grace Underhill McElroy charged into the room, her hair askew, her eyes wild. Her angry gaze swept the room, coming to rest on Olivia. "Where is he? Where's James? I want to see him," Grace said, tears streaking her carefully applied foundation and leaving lumps of mascara clinging to her cheeks.

CHAPTER FOUR

RELIEF SURGED through Olivia as she hugged her friend. "James took sick last night and he's had emergency heart surgery. He's in Intensive Care," Olivia said, her spirits lifting at the sight of her friend, someone who knew how long she and James had waited for their happiness.

"Why didn't you call me?" Grace asked, a frown marring her flawless forehead as she held Olivia at arm's length and stared into her eyes.

"I didn't get a chance. James got sick so quickly, and all I could think of was getting him to the hospital. Who called you?"

"Your illustrious mother-in-law, who else?" Grace shrugged her elegant shoulders, reminding Olivia of how awful she must look in contrast. She was wearing the old jeans and turtleneck sweater she'd pulled on before leaving with James in the ambulance.

Silly and petty, she admitted, but Grace and James had once been married, and Olivia couldn't help wondering, especially today, whether Grace and James would still be married if things had happened differently. Susan McElroy had never made any secret of her preference in the matter.

Yet, despite Susan's interference, Olivia and Grace were still friends. "I'm glad she called you," Olivia said. "Let's sit down and talk while we wait to hear from the nursing staff." She linked arms with Grace and led the way to a comfortable spot by the window.

"Wait for the nursing staff? You mean something *more* has gone wrong?" Grace asked, her body rigid against the chair.

"No, I'm only allowed to visit him for short periods of time, at the discretion of the nursing staff."

"Well, the nurses aren't the ones in charge, it's the doctor. Have you talked to him?"

"Yes, and he thinks James may have a clotting problem, on top of the open-heart surgery."

"A what?" Grace rose from the chair and headed for the door. "Where is this doctor? I want to talk to him," Grace demanded, her voice rising. "I have a right to know what's going on with James."

Surprised at Grace's reaction, Olivia said, "You're concerned about James, of course, but the doctor's already talked to his family—"

"You mean you, right?" Grace shot back, her

hands on her hips, while two points of color competed with the rouge on her cheeks.

What was Grace doing? "I mean that the doctor has talked to Susan McElroy and me," Olivia said, trying for a calmness she didn't feel.

Grace fidgeted with the gold watch on her narrow wrist, a clear indication that she needed a cigarette.

"I'm sorry, Olivia. I didn't mean to be so rude, but I'm worried about James. I know you understand." Grace opened her large black bag, her shoulders tense as she pulled a pack of cigarettes from amid the clutter.

Grace had become a part of their lives again. After she and James divorced, Grace disappeared for a couple of years. They'd heard rumors about her wild lifestyle and her stint as an interior designer for one of the hotel chains. After Olivia and James were married, Grace did everything she could to show them that she valued their friendship. At first, Olivia was suspicious of Grace's intentions where her husband was concerned, but Grace had been so supportive of Olivia's relationship with James that Olivia had ignored her worries about Grace's motives.

Now, as she watched Grace trying to take control, she wasn't so sure. "I know you didn't mean to be rude. And I know you care about James, but you really don't need to be here."

"Be here? Why wouldn't I be here? With my two best friends." Grace gestured around the empty room. "Are you alone?"

"Yes, but it's okay. I want to be able to see James anytime they'll allow me in the room."

"Well, you're not alone now," Grace said, smoothing the hair from her face. Cigarette in one hand, she searched for an ashtray.

"Grace, you can't smoke in the hospital." Olivia pointed to the No Smoking sign posted on the wall.

Grace returned to the chair beside Olivia, her emaciated shoulders sagging under the gold silk blouse she wore. "I want to see James. I have to see for myself that he's okay."

Resentment brewed in Olivia. "Grace, you're being unreasonable."

Grace glanced up at Olivia, tears shimmering in her eyes. "I know we're divorced, and I know you and I have been over all this before, but—"

"Grace, I will keep you informed, but you can't go in to see him. It's family only."

Grace, her lips set in a determined line, faced Olivia. "I *am* going to see him. I want to be involved in his care."

"Grace, please don't. This is not about you. It's about a very ill man who is my husband, and I will make the decisions about his welfare. You have no role to play, except to be my friend…if you want to."

Grace stared at her for a moment. "I am your friend."

"Then act like it. I want you here with me, but not if you're going to insist on seeing my husband."

Grace's eyes were dark. "Hearing that James is ill made me realize that nothing's changed for me. And it never will. I need James in my life. If I'd been able to have a child—"

"Don't say that."

Grace had never stopped obsessing over her belief that a child would have saved her marriage. Olivia knew only too well that nothing could save a marriage if one partner didn't want to be in it.

Tears clung to Grace's eyelashes. "It's easy for you to say. You have everything, including a son."

"Grace! Stop this right now."

A son. Grace's heated words brought back memories of the day Kyle was born.

"He's perfect, isn't he?" Alex said, his voice filled with fondness, his eyes alight with pleasure.

Olivia held her son against her chest, soaking in the warmth of his tiny form and smoothing the cap of dark hair on his head—James's dark hair. "Oh, yes, he is," she whispered, the pain of the past difficult hours slipping into obscurity.

Alex leaned over and kissed her forehead. "Kyle Alexander Crawford is a lucky little boy."

"And I'm lucky, too," she murmured, touching Alex's cheek. "Thanks for being here for me. I couldn't have made it through without you."

She'd never been so terrified in her life. When the labor pains got so bad that all she could do was beg to be put to sleep, the doctor had told her to keep pushing. And through it all, Alex had waited patiently outside the delivery room.

"I'll always be there for you."

Olivia smiled as he pulled a chair up close to the bed. She was so thankful to have Alex, who made her feel pampered and cared for—all the nice things men do for the women they love. "Always is a long time, Alex."

"Not nearly long enough for me," he said, taking a jeweler's box from his coat pocket. With a smile of satisfaction on his face, he opened the velvet box to reveal a ring of gold with three diamonds in it.

"I'm calling this our family ring. Three stones for now, and more can be added when we have children of our own."

He slid the ring onto her finger, the stones sparkling under the fluorescent lights. "It's beautiful, really beautiful," Olivia said, tucking the baby into the crook of her arm and turning her hand for a better look at the ring.

Seeing it reminded her of another ring, hidden in her jewelry box.

"But not nearly as beautiful as you," Alex said, his gaze meeting hers. "I can't wait to get you and Kyle home to our house and the new nursery. In the meantime, I want you to rest as much as you can. I'm hiring someone to come in and help you. Mom's offered to interview people for us."

"I want to look after Kyle."

"Relax, honey. Mom knows everybody in town, and she'll choose the best possible person. Besides, it's her gift to Kyle. He'll have a nanny for a year."

Talking about Alex's mother made Olivia cringe. Olivia had no intention of causing any trouble, but she really wanted to make a family life for Kyle without having to constantly fend off Caroline Crawford.

"Alex, are you sure she doesn't suspect something? I wish we'd told your mother the truth about Kyle."

"You leave my mother to me. She's going to accept Kyle as if he were her flesh-and-blood grandson, and so are the people of Bar Harbor."

"How can you be so sure?"

"You were almost a month late. And no one will question what I say. If they do, I'll tell them we met in Boston—whatever it takes to make Kyle's life perfect. Besides, there's no way my mother or anyone else will ever believe this isn't my child when they see us together," he said, easing the sleeping infant from her arms and carrying him around the room.

Alex was probably right. They'd been careful to maintain the story that this child was his. Yet a part of Olivia wanted to tell somebody about Kyle, about Kyle's real father. Tears dripped from her lashes.

"Ah, honey, you're not going to cry, are you?" Alex asked, easing the baby into the bassinet.

Coming around the end of the bed, he took her hand in his. "Everything will be all right. Soon you're going to be home with our son and someone to help you take care of him."

He raised her chin and wiped a stray tear from her cheek. "I'm going to take good care of you. I have to go to the office, but I'll be back."

His words flooded her heart with the memory of the last words James had ever said to her, the promise that he'd return.

He hadn't meant a word of it. For nearly a year, he'd let her live in the hope that he would come back to her, a false hope that now held only despair.

But while James had failed her, Alex had been there for her, for her son. Alex was a wonderful man who deserved a good life with a woman who loved him. She might not love him right now, but with the birth of Kyle, anything was possible.

Olivia smiled at her husband, pushing away the thoughts going through her head and the unease in her heart.

She had one choice, and it was to make a life with Alex, and forget what might have been. Kyle deserved the best family life she could give him.

Heedless of the tears flowing over her cheeks, Olivia closed her eyes and remembered her dream, the one that had died when James walked out of her life.

She'd known the dream was dead when Alex, not James, had been the one to hold Kyle for the first time. James hadn't seen his son's birth or heard his first cries.

After she'd married Alex, Olivia had not spoken James's name to anyone. But James was with her, as if he hadn't left, and never more so than in the last few hours. She wanted to be angry with him for what he'd done. But it was anger born of loneliness and longing.

Because no matter how hard she tried, she couldn't blot out her hope that someday, somehow, James would return for her and their son.

But none of that mattered anymore. Kyle would become the focus of her life. Kyle would have everything she could give him, including a stable home.

Kyle would never know that he wasn't Alex's son, or that his real father had abandoned his mother.

A YEAR LATER, Olivia stood staring out the nursery window early one evening, the phone still in her hands and her chest tight from the words she hadn't said to Alex's mother.

Caroline Crawford had scolded her because of the way she'd dressed Kyle for his morning outing—for not putting his snowsuit on in the middle of April!

Caroline's words stung as they always did. Regardless of the fact that Olivia and Alex now lived in their new home, miles down the coast from Caroline, she continued to judge everything Olivia did when it came to Kyle. Sarah, the nanny, reported all her so-called infractions to Caroline who then criticized Olivia for them.

Olivia had more than her share of insecurities as a new mother, and Caroline's constant criticism exacerbated those feelings. Olivia had put her mother-in-law's demands down to her loneliness, but being a widow didn't excuse her behavior.

If only she and Alex were free to enjoy Kyle in their own way. She wanted so much to include Alex in every aspect of Kyle's life, from feeding to bedtime stories. But to do this, she had to remind Sarah that *she* was Kyle's mother, and that she'd look after him.

Her mood lightened when she saw Kyle being carried from his bath by Sarah, dark curls framing his pink cheeks. "I'll take him," she said, holding out her arms.

Frowning, Sarah passed Kyle to her, and Olivia began to towel-dry his velvety skin. She never failed to marvel at how perfect he was, from his toes to the tiny dimples in his cheeks. His gurgling laughter and his plump fingers patting her arm wiped away any thoughts of his grandmother.

"Well, if it isn't my two favorite people in all the world," Alex said, striding into the nursery, his smile making Olivia's world so much better.

"Isn't he sweet," she murmured against Alex's mouth as he kissed her, his clean-scrubbed scent reminding her of how safe she felt when he was with her. Safe and cared for, and somehow that had to be enough.

"He's sweet, all right." Alex touched Kyle's cheek. "Did I mention that Mom's making arrangements for his christening next month?"

Knowing Sarah could hear them, Olivia lowered her voice. "Alex, we need to talk about your mother. I just got off the phone with her."

"You know Mom means well."

"I'm not so sure, and Sarah's just a pipeline back to her." Olivia hated the whining tone in her voice.

Alex sighed. "Mom can be a little overbearing at times."

"But, Alex, this is *our* life and my child—" Olivia heard her words, and flushed at the realization of what she'd said.

"You mean our child, don't you?" Alex countered, his voice tinged with recrimination.

"Yes, of course I do," she said too quickly.

"Olivia, I'm Kyle's father in every way that matters," he whispered, peeking over his shoulder to see where Sarah was.

"Of course you are, and I want us to be a family," she whispered back.

There was silence between them as Olivia stared up at Alex. How could she have said something so stupid and insensitive?

"I didn't mean to make it sound like you weren't." She reached for him, her hands clutching the smooth cotton of his shirt.

He nodded and his fingers folded over hers. "Kyle is our son. My mother loves Kyle, and she wants to be part of his life. I agree that makes things difficult for us at times, but—"

"I realize she loves Kyle," Olivia broke in, "but I wish it was just you, me and Kyle."

"Give Mom time to adjust…"

"She's had over a year, for heaven's sake!"

"She's alone. She has no one but us," he answered.

Olivia hated to be ungenerous, but her mother-in-law's involvement in their lives was becoming intolerable. And there was nothing she could do about it.

CHAPTER FIVE

IN MANY WAYS the next three years flew past, but in other ways it was as if time had stood still. Olivia still read the Boston Globe from front to back, looking for any reference to James. There wasn't any, but his father had become a member of several prestigious boards, and his mother's picture was often shown in relation to her fundraising efforts for various charities.

And each day, her delight in Kyle grew, a delight that kept memories of James alive in her heart.

Kyle's smile reminded her of James. She remembered how James had believed she could do anything she set her mind to. Seeing Kyle's excitement over his toy train reminded Olivia how much she missed James's enthusiasm, his insistence that anything was possible.

And she missed her friends, as well. Especially in the early hours when she went out for a run before Kyle woke up. In those quiet moments she reminisced about all the people who were no longer part of her life.

Her parents phoned once a week, but other than that, she had no contact with her past. Her aunt and uncle had retired to Florida. Not since the day Olivia got on the bus for Bar Harbor, had she contacted Grace. She hadn't invited her to the wedding because she was afraid Grace would figure out that Olivia was pregnant with James's child, not Alex's.

She still thought of Grace as a friend, but couldn't be sure that she wouldn't tell people about her sudden marriage. It wouldn't take long for the people back in Frampton to draw the obvious conclusions…. Olivia had already lost the life she'd planned with James; she couldn't face losing her dignity along with it. Yet she missed Grace so much, and often wondered if she was enjoying college.

Despite her disappointment over her own college plans, Olivia's life was pleasant. Kyle was an energetic little boy who needed love and attention, which he got from both of his parents. Now that the nanny was finally out of their lives, Olivia had a sense of freedom she hadn't experienced since before Kyle was born.

It was a Friday morning in May. As she rounded the bend of the circular drive, she remembered the first day they'd moved into their new home. It'd been fun to decorate the house, picking paint colors and looking for furniture.

But the lawns and flower beds were her special interest, along with the vegetable garden she maintained despite Alex's protestations about the amount of work it entailed. The rose hedge she'd planted near the patio doors thrived in the sea air. The view from the front lawns was spectacular, a vista of tiny islands fanning out from the shore.

She had taken this run a hundred mornings since they'd moved into the huge bungalow on the crest of the hill, but today felt different, filled with promise.

Her excitement came from an idea Olivia had about what she wanted to do with her life. Spotting Alex out on the patio with a cup of coffee, she ran to him.

"Wow, what a lovely day for a run. Tomorrow you'll have to come with me," she said, pouring a glass of juice.

Alex patted his abdomen. "I should exercise, for sure."

"I'll drag you kicking and screaming out of bed, and I'll race you from here to the restaurant and back. Be prepared for me to win," she said, smiling with contentment.

"I accept," Alex said, returning her smile.

Seeing Alex in a good mood sent shivers of relief through Olivia. In the past months, Alex had been withdrawn and distant. He still took great pleasure in Kyle but seldom shared in the little boy's care, saying that Olivia was better at it than he was.

Alex no longer confided his work problems in her, the way he used to. He'd begun staying up late and watching TV. Then, in the morning, he'd be tired and out of sorts. Work pressures, she wanted to believe, but Alex never seemed to have time for a social life unless it was business-related, a niggling worry that had Olivia searching for ways to make their life together more enjoyable.

She took heart from the idea that what she had planned would help him get over his preoccupation with work.

"Running in the morning would be a great way for us to start our day, and I had a brilliant idea while I was out running this morning," she said, sliding into the chair across from him.

"Oh? Am I about to get another suggestion from my lovely wife on how to run my business?"

Was that condescension she heard in his voice? "Yes, as a matter of fact, you are."

Alex sat forward, a hint of a frown on his face. "I'm listening."

"I'm going back to work, managing the restaurant."

"Why?"

"I've been thinking about it, and I know it's right for me. I loved working at the restaurant, and I miss it. I miss having a life of my own, something I can enjoy."

"You don't enjoy looking after Kyle? I thought that's what you wanted."

"Of course I do, but he'll be going to kindergarten soon. And it would be so nice to have an outside interest. You said yourself that I was good at managing the restaurant."

"And you're good at being Kyle's mother."

"But I need more."

Alex's jaw flexed as he settled back in the chair. "I don't get it. First, you want me to let Sarah go so you can take care of Kyle. And now you want to leave him to go to work."

Knowing where this argument was headed, Olivia stifled a sigh. Whenever Olivia tried to talk about how quiet her life was, despite her love of caring for Kyle, he fell back on the old response that he appreciated her being a stay-at-home mom. Alex's business success had made him a pillar of the community, something he relished. As the wife of a successful man, she had no financial need to work outside the home.

"Alex, I've got a lead on a woman who could look after Kyle while I'm at the restaurant. I want to go back to work, back to helping you."

"Take a course, or learn a craft, like other women do." He tossed the words at her as he snapped open the paper and spread it out on the table.

The first intimations of anger threaded their way through Olivia's mind. "I'm not 'other women.' I'm your wife. I want to be part of your business life, like I was before."

"Did you ask me if that's what *I* wanted?" His voice had an edge to it Olivia had never heard.

Past experience told her that this discussion was in danger of turning into another argument in which Alex blamed everything that was wrong with modern life on the women's liberation movement. In an effort to stave off the usual conclusion, she gentled her tone. "Before I realized I was pregnant, I had a full scholarship to Hastings College. I planned to have a career. That plan was delayed, not abandoned."

Alex stared at her, his dark eyes filled with a reproach that made Olivia feel guilty. And feeling guilty about wanting to work, to be independent, made her remember James, and their excited discussions about careers. With James there'd never been any question about her ability, nor any doubt that she'd be an equal partner in their relationship.

As the arguments with Alex had escalated in the past months, comparisons between Alex and James were becoming a more frequent part of her life—something that brought with it a sense of dread. There had to be a way to get Alex to understand how she felt about having a career.

"Alex, I don't want to argue about this, but I would like you to hear me out."

He sighed, but said nothing.

"Please, will you at least consider it?" she pleaded, knowing that as kind and thoughtful as Alex could be, there was always this feeling that because he was fifteen years older than Olivia, his decisions carried more weight.

Alex glanced at her. "Olivia, I have to get to the office. Can we talk about this next week, after I get back from Detroit?" Alex took her hand in his, an action that usually soothed Olivia. "I see how important it is to you, honey, but can it wait? At least until next week?"

Typical of Alex—when he didn't want to do something, he postponed the decision, hoping that the problem would go away on its own. It made her sad to think that he didn't really want to know what made her happy—only what made *him* happy and a success in the eyes of those who mattered in Bar Harbor.

But Olivia couldn't let this go. Over the past

months she'd come to the realization that something was missing in her life. Somehow, she had to convince him that a career was important to her. Maybe what they needed was a night out, a chance to reconnect. "Sure, it can wait, if you feel it has to. Why don't we go out to dinner tonight?"

"Are we celebrating something? You're not pregnant, are you?"

She saw the hope in his eyes, and wished she could provide him with the answer he so wanted. "No, we're going out on a date—the way we used to. Let's go to a disco and dance. Why don't we call Earle and Linda and see if they'd like to come with us?"

"I'm too old for discos, and besides, Mom asked us to come to dinner tonight. When she heard I was going to be out of town on business, she suggested we bring Kyle over for a visit."

Olivia pressed her lips together in frustration. "Why didn't you tell me?"

"I forgot. She called me at the office. She wants to talk about sending Kyle to a private school. She's already searched out all the best ones in the area and would like us to help her decide which one would give him the most advantages. Mom plans to make her contribution to Kyle's schooling by paying the tuition."

Betrayal and hurt dominated Olivia's thoughts

as she stared at her husband. "Your mother will never stop trying to run our lives, will she?"

Alex frowned and looked away. "Olivia, don't do this. I'm going away tomorrow and I'd hoped we could have a relaxing evening."

Would her husband ever stand up to his mother? When hell froze over, probably. Olivia sighed inwardly.

Today had begun on such a positive note.

But what happened this morning had become a pattern. Olivia would be excited about an idea and Alex would pour cold water on it, or imply that she didn't know what she was talking about. Or worse still, announce yet another of his mother's interfering plans.

"Why is your mother involved in choosing a school for Kyle? And last I checked, we didn't need your mother's money."

"Mom only has you and me and Kyle for family," he told her, not for the first time. "It makes sense that she'd want Kyle to have the best of everything. She's so alone, surely we can be generous with her on this?"

"Alex, your mother's behavior goes way beyond being a grandmother. She wants to run our lives and Kyle's," she said.

"Now you're being unfair. Mom isn't getting

any younger, and Kyle's the only grandchild she has." He gave her a knowing look.

"Alex, I will not negotiate with your mother on this. Kyle is not going to be sent away to a private school. I couldn't bear to have him leave, and I'm not willing to discuss it."

LATER THE next evening, Olivia sat on the edge of the tub, bathing Kyle and listening to his squeals of delight as he splashed in the warm water. Kyle's bath time was one of her favorite parts of the day.

She watched Kyle, her mind on Alex and his mother. They'd canceled dinner with his mother, but Alex had been quiet and withdrawn all evening. When he left this morning, he'd hardly said goodbye.

Nothing had been resolved with regard to Caroline's plans for Kyle's schooling. Alex had agreed not to go to dinner at his mother's, but that was all.

With the argument between her and Alex still ringing in her ears, she smiled at Kyle as he grabbed his plastic duck from the rack of toys strung across the tub and splashed water all over her, giving her a mischievous grin and clapping his hands in glee.

"You're getting Mommy all wet." She pretended to scold him as she scooped the facecloth from the water and scrubbed the remnants of peanut butter from his rosy cheeks.

"No," he howled, pushing her hand away.

"Time to get out, you little monkey," she said, lifting his sturdy body onto the towel spread in her lap.

"More," Kyle demanded. He stuck his thumb in his mouth and scowled up at her.

"Not tonight, my Pooh bear. You've had enough for one day." She toweled him dry, feeling a surge of love for her son that was as welcome as it was overwhelming. The flood of feeling comforted her as she took him to his room.

"There you go," she said. She put him on his bed, then pulled fresh pajamas from the drawer.

With four fingers jammed in his mouth, he watched as she dressed him for bed, his grin matching hers when she picked him up and cuddled him in her arms.

"Mommy's going to read to you," she whispered into the clean scent of his hair. She carried him to the maple rocker in a corner of the room. Settling in, she drew a book from the pile on the table beside the rocker and smiled with pleasure as his tiny hands grasped it. Her heart rose in her chest at the sight of him in her arms, the way his lashes rested on his round cheeks, the way his dark eyes stared up at her.

Kyle looked more like James with each passing day, making her sad at what had been lost. James would never have the chance to experience what she was experiencing now as their son lay in her arms, his pudgy hands holding his book. With regret holding her thoughts captive, she began to read to him, waiting as she always did for his eyes to cloud over with sleep.

But Kyle was so fortunate to have Alex as his father. Alex had provided a safe haven for her son—and for her—from the moment he'd learned about her pregnancy. During the months she'd worked in the restaurant, he'd kept her secret, and made it clear that he was there for her in every possible way. After Kyle was born, Alex had been an adoring father. He played with him, talked baby talk to him, and bragged to everyone about Kyle's accomplishments.

But recently, Olivia had begun to worry that Kyle might grow up missing something by not having the chance to be with James.

James would have loved his son with all his heart; she was sure of it. He would've played with him, carried him on his shoulders and grinned in glee as Kyle took his first steps.

In her need to protect Kyle, had she made a terrible mistake?

She wished she could tell James about his son. But her courage always failed her in the presence of what he—and his family—might do.

What if they tried to take Kyle from her?

Would James want to be Kyle's father, or had he made a whole new life that couldn't possibly include his son? And if she told him, and he made no attempt to get to know his son, how would she survive the rejection? Could she handle the tragedy her life would become if the father of her son didn't want him?

And what would Alex do, how would he feel? Despite their differences, Olivia couldn't hurt Alex. He loved Kyle; she had no doubt of that. He was a good man, and it wasn't his fault that she didn't love him.

Deep in her soul, she knew that she didn't belong in Alex's life. There was no connection between them. They'd had no chance to learn about each other without the urgent need her situation had created. She suspected that Alex had married her out of guilt for his past, not real love for her. Despite that, he was frequently kind and always generous.

But he wasn't James. He hadn't been part of her life at a time when anything was possible, when everything was a new, exciting experience. Alex didn't understand her need to be accepted, to test her abilities in the world.

Alex wanted a wife who fit the mold his mother had cast.

Olivia wanted a husband who appreciated her for who she was, what she could do.

Olivia did her best to ignore the feeling that she didn't really belong to Alex's world, and on nights like this, when she was alone, her longing for James welled up in her.

With Kyle in her life, and her almost desperate need to make her marriage work, Olivia hadn't developed any close friendships in Bar Harbor. But she recognized the reason for not becoming involved with other women her age.

She missed her old life, her friends from the past. To forget her past life was to abandon her memories.

Trying not to wake Kyle, she eased out of the rocker and brought him to his bed. He frowned, his lips moving in a pout as he settled into bed.

Pulling the quilt her mother had made for him over his shoulders, she kissed the downy softness of his head, and tiptoed out of the room.

Down in the kitchen, she tidied the counters and filled the dishwasher and still her thoughts clung to James, and what he might be doing tonight. She could no longer deny her persistent need to talk to him, to tell him what had happened and the miracle that was their son.

She glanced at the phone, wanting to call him, to hear his voice, to ease the desire to know what his life was like now.

Would he want to hear from her?

Insecurity paralyzed her for a moment. What kind of trouble would she cause now if she called the McElroy house? She remembered all too well what they'd threatened to do.

She glanced at the phone again. Before she could talk herself out of it, she dialed the McElroy house, a number she knew from memory. She'd never called his home when they were seeing each other, but she'd memorized it recently—because of all the nights she'd considered doing this.

The phone was answered on the first ring. A woman's voice reached across the line.

"Could I please speak to James?" Olivia ventured.

"He's in Ireland. This is his mother. May I ask who's calling?"

"When do you expect him back?" Olivia asked, trying to steady her hand where it gripped the phone.

"James isn't due back anytime soon. Who's this?"

Should she tell Mrs. McElroy who she was? It had been over four years. Surely the woman couldn't bear a grudge that long? "Mrs. McElroy, this is Olivia Banks. I…need to talk to James," she said, her voice struggling against the trapped air in her lungs.

"I'm sorry. Who did you say was calling?"

"It's Olivia Banks. James's…friend."

There was a pause, then the words burst out.

"You, young lady, are no friend of my son. You're the reason he had to leave home. You are not part of James's life, and you have no business calling here."

Olivia cringed at the heartless words, but she couldn't let the woman get away with saying something so cruel. "What did I do to make you say such a thing?"

"What did you *do?* You pretended to love my son. You made him lie to protect you. You made him get his sister to keep the truth from us. My son should've been able to stay here and go to college as he planned. Your scheming to get him to marry you left my husband no choice but to send him away."

"That's not true! None of it. I would never do anything to hurt James. I loved him. And he loved me."

"Maybe he *thought* he loved you, but look what it cost him—and us," she said, her words laced with anger.

Fear spiked through Olivia at the possibility of what Susan McElroy would do when she got off the phone. If she told her husband, and he acted on his earlier threat, he might do something to her parents. How much trouble had she made for them by talking to this woman?

And if Alex found out…

Fear scuttled her courage. "I won't bother you again, Mrs. McElroy." She hung up the phone.

CHAPTER SIX

JAMES STARED out the narrow window of his office in Dublin, watching the rain stream over the glass, his thoughts on Olivia. He'd gone over that night in the school parking lot a thousand times, and each time, regret overwhelmed him. He should have told Olivia the whole truth. He should've explained that his ribs were bruised and one broken from the blow that sent him into the mahogany desk in his father's office. He should've stood his ground and insisted on bringing Olivia with him. Or refused to obey his father and fended for himself. With Olivia...

Instead, he'd abandoned her that night with little or nothing to believe in, except that he would be back.

He'd just gotten off the phone with his sister, Julia. She'd defied her father and dropped out of the college he'd insisted she attend after she graduated from Frampton High a year ago.

She was living in New York, working in a restaurant to support herself, and taking night classes in psychology at NYU. She sounded so happy, so in control of her life. She'd fought hard for her independence, and he was delighted to hear about her happiness.

So what the hell was wrong with him? He'd done what his father demanded, and yet his life was still in limbo.

It was five years since he'd seen Olivia. He had no idea where she'd gone; all he knew for sure was that she hadn't gone to Hastings College and, as far as he could tell, she hadn't stayed in Frampton. He'd called her parents' home, only to be rebuffed by her mother. His letters were returned unopened. Olivia had disappeared, almost certainly with her parents' help.

James had called Directory Assistance for every city from New York to Bangor. He couldn't locate a listing for Olivia anywhere. The private detective he'd hired had searched for any public record of Olivia in the State of Massachusetts, and had called her parents, who'd refused to talk to him. The detective was still looking for Olivia, but James hadn't heard from him in months.

What would have driven her to hide from him? Had she changed so much? Had she stopped loving him? But what right did he have to expect her to wait all this time?

Just after Thanksgiving, two years ago, he'd called his friend Sean to see if he knew anything about Olivia, but Sean was doing a tour of duty in Vietnam and not expected back for another six months. James hadn't qualified for the draft because of his heart murmur, but that didn't stop him from wishing he'd been able to go.

Anything to feel better about himself, and what he'd done to Olivia.

He yearned to hear her laughter, to touch her. He remembered the way her eyes would light up whenever he teased her. The way her hair shone in the sunlight. The way she ate fried clams with such gusto. The long walks along the lake while they talked about their future together.

He would always remember, yet some part of him accepted that Olivia had moved on with her life. And during those dark lonely nights, he would wonder where she was, try to imagine what she was doing.

Only his work gave him any sense of satisfaction. He'd discovered that he had an intuitive understanding of all the new electronics his uncle's firm was manufacturing.

"Hello, there. Want to go to lunch?" his uncle Seamus McElroy called out from the doorway.

James turned from the window, meeting his uncle's inquiring smile. Seamus, a towering man of over six feet tall, put the fear of God into a lot of people when they first met him. But most of the staff at Laurel Industries, the parent company of McElroy Manufacturing, at which his uncle was president and chief executive officer, were on to the fact that under his brusque exterior hid a kind heart.

Laurel Industries had begun as a producer of fine woven cottons and linens, and had expanded into the States when James's father moved there. As soon as an opportunity to get into the electronics industry in Ireland presented itself, Laurel Industries, under Seamus's capable leadership, became a leader in marine electronics.

For James, Seamus was father and uncle rolled into one.

From the moment James had arrived in Dublin, lonely and homesick, Seamus had made him feel welcome. He'd taken the time to initiate James into the companies he ran through Laurel Industries, ranging from highly sophisticated transistor development and production to marine communication equipment. His uncle made a point of introducing him to the business world of Dublin as if James were an equal.

His father had never treated James that way, so it took a little getting used to. Still an experience that had started out as the worst in James's life had been saved by Seamus.

"I'd love a bite of lunch," James said.

"Then grab your raincoat and let's go."

They made it to the elevator just before the doors closed, and stood packed in the crowded space as it whizzed toward the ground floor. Several women met James's glance, offering him smiles of encouragement as he looked around at the passengers standing there so quietly.

When the elevator slid open, he and Seamus strode together through the marble lobby to the front doors of the building owned by his uncle.

"Did you get a look at the dark-haired darling giving you the eye back there?" his uncle asked, nodding at the cabbie waiting by the curb. "Or is your mind still on that overseas contract?" He gave the cabbie the address of his men's club on Fleet Street near the Temple Bar area of the city.

"The contract. I sent it back to the legal department for a review of some of the patent requirements," James said.

"Women aren't on the agenda, is that it?"

Much as he wanted to confide in his uncle, he hadn't. He wasn't sure whether or not his uncle would tell his father that he still had feelings for Olivia. "Something like that."

"Am I working you so hard you haven't the energy to date some of these women?" his uncle asked, one bushy eyebrow cocked.

"I like my work."

"Don't ignore women for too long. That's my advice."

"I hear you."

The cab pulled away from the curb, into the traffic, giving James a chance to change the subject. "I intend to learn everything I can about Laurel Industries before I'm through."

"Well, I can tell you, son, you've surprised the hell out of me. You're better than a lot of the high-priced staff I've hired. You have a gift for the design side of electronics, and I'd like to see you do a degree in electrical engineering. You have the talent and the brains for it."

"Tell that to my father," James muttered, gazing out the rain-washed window.

"My brother's a tough old goat, but it's nothing personal. Our father was a mean bastard and your father, being the oldest, had to be an obedient and trustworthy son. That's how he ended up going to the United States—our father's orders."

"Pretty rotten way to live, if you ask me."

"He had no choice. 'Either do as you're told or get out' was our father's creed. In the end, your dad embraced the idea. And, as you well know, he's been that way with everyone ever since—except when it comes to businesspeople. He seems to be able to charm them," his uncle reflected wryly.

"My father charming? I find that a little hard to believe," James said as the cab arrived at the club where he and his uncle ate their Friday lunch.

"Believe you me, I've seen him in action. When he's making a deal, he can charm the birds out of the trees," his uncle said. They moved up the steps to the restaurant doors, shaking water off their raincoats.

Passing their coats to the doorman, they went straight to their favorite table. His uncle rubbed his hands in anticipation as he surveyed the tables arranged in front of huge, towering windows and a fireplace tall enough to walk into.

"This is the kind of day made for fried fish and Guinness, wouldn't you agree?"

"That's what you have every Friday."

His uncle chuckled, a rich, delighted sound that James enjoyed. "You're telling me I'm a creature of habit?"

"That I am."

They sat down across from each other, sinking into the worn leather of the large, comfortable chairs. Several people came by the table to speak to Seamus, and James eyed his uncle with affection.

He wanted to thank him for everything he'd done, but Seamus would brush off any show of appreciation on James's part, saying he had simply done right by family. But for James it went so much further than that.

"You look like you have something on your mind today," his uncle noted.

James tucked his tie carefully inside his suit jacket. "Yeah, I do. I was thinking how different my life has been since I came to Ireland. I dreaded coming here."

"But you made out all right."

"Thanks to you. I would never have survived if you hadn't been so kind to me."

"We've been through this before," his uncle said, "and I understand how hard it was for you to leave home. I've had the feeling in the last couple of days that there's something else you want to talk about."

Leave it to his Uncle Seamus to jump right in. James smiled to ease the tension building up in him. "I…I miss my girlfriend."

"Ah, so that's what this is about. Go on."

"I suppose Dad told you I was sent here for going out with someone my parents didn't consider suitable."

"No, he didn't say what the infraction was, but I guessed. You were moping around, and that's why I dumped so much work on you in the beginning. Thought I could bring you out of yourself."

"And you did."

"So, now what?"

"Now, I'd like to go back for Olivia."

"So that's her name." His uncle nodded approvingly, his heavy eyebrows pulled together in concentration.

"Yeah, I went to school with her. She and I are in love…or at least we were."

His uncle squinted at him for a couple of minutes, then tapped the table as if making up his mind. "Son, I hope you don't think I'm interfering here, but I've been where you are, and I can tell you what I'd do."

"What do you mean?"

"Your aunt Celia, my dear wife, was the love of my life. She was the prettiest woman for miles around, and everyone loved her, including me. Not only did I love her, I couldn't live without her. My situation was like yours—my father laid down the law. I was not to see her under any circumstances. None of my family wanted me anywhere near her, including your dad."

"What did you do?"

"Nothing. She became a matron at the hospital a few miles from here, living her life for the joy of being kind to others. I moped around, ended up not marrying anyone. Then, one day I went into the hospital where she worked, and I ran into her. In those few heart-wrenching moments we knew.

By then I was a wealthy man, and enough of a person in my own right and I no longer needed my family's approval. I married Celia."

"And lived happily?" He knew Seamus had been a widower for a decade or more.

"Not exactly. Celia was diagnosed with cancer soon after. We had two years, four months and seventeen days together."

"Oh, God."

"We had such plans, such hopes for our future. And then…nothing. Losing my dear Celia was the worst time in my life."

His uncle's eyes shone with unshed tears. "If you truly love this woman, then take your father on. He'll fight you, and you'll wonder if it's worth it. But in the end…"

James watched as the waiter placed two tall glasses of Guinness on the table.

"You don't know my father like I do. I've never won an argument with him in my life."

"And you're afraid you won't win this one, either."

"I know I won't." James let the air he'd been holding in his lungs slip away. "My father will never accept Olivia."

"Then maybe you have to make your decision based on what *you* need."

"And lose my family?"

His uncle placed his hand on James's arm. "I understand how frightening the thought of losing your family can be. But if they won't accept who you are, and who you love, do you have a choice?"

"I don't think I could face down my father that way."

"Why? He doesn't run your life. You're independent—and making good money, I might add."

Why couldn't he confront his father, man-to-man, and explain what he wanted in his life? Was he such a coward that he'd let his father continue to call the shots? But if he defied him, what would be the consequences for Olivia's parents?

He remembered the first time he'd tried to stand up to his father…. He was ten years old and wanted a new bike. His father said that a new bike was frivolous, and no son of his would ever waste money on such things.

His father had hit him so hard he broke his arm.

James looked at his uncle, and wished, again, that this man had been his father. "I would, just once, like my father to have a little faith in me. And accept me for who I am, not for what he wants me to be."

"Even if it means giving up on someone you love?"

"I'm not going to give up on her. I can't. She means everything to me."

"So, what are you going to do about it?"

"I need to talk to Olivia."

"Where is she?"

"That's the problem. I don't know."

"Then maybe you should go home and find her, see how she feels about you."

"We've loved each other for a long time."

His uncle's expression softened. "You have, have you?" he asked, his voice gentle.

"Yes, but almost five years have gone by."

"And you're afraid that her feelings have changed. That you've lost your chance with her by coming here, that she's better off without you. You know something, James? A man who can't stand up to his father wouldn't make much of a husband." He paused, shaking his head. "Like I said, I've been there."

James decided then and there, that no matter what he did with his life, his uncle would never know a moment of pain or worry if James could prevent it. "Thanks for understanding."

"But what I don't understand is why you didn't tell me this before."

"I was afraid you didn't appreciate how difficult my situation was. After all, you're my father's brother."

"And brothers share the same blood, right?"

"I guess that's it." James gave his uncle a

rueful smile. Finally, for the first time in a long while, he didn't feel completely alone in his need to find Olivia.

Seamus wrapped his big hand around the glass of stout as he fixed his gaze on James. "I want you to follow your heart, and if that means searching for this girl and bringing her into your life, so be it." He lifted his glass. "To happiness."

Filled with hope and a sense of purpose, James raised his glass. "To happiness."

CHAPTER SEVEN

KYLE'S FOURTH birthday dawned bright and sunny, and Olivia felt on top of the world. She was in the kitchen putting the finishing touches on his chocolate birthday cake when she heard a squeal of laughter coming from the family room.

"What are you doing, sweetness?" she asked, putting the bowls in the sink.

Kyle raced into the kitchen with his Pooh Bear under his arm and a smile on his face that brought joy to Olivia's heart. She scooped him into her arms and kissed his velvety cheek.

"You're Mama's best boy, did you know that?"

He patted her face with one plump little hand and placed his nose on hers. "I'm *your* Pooh Bear," he whispered, his dark eyes so much like James's.

He had his father's charm and looks, and James would never know any of it. Regret made her heart thud rapidly against her ribs.

The door chimes played. "Down," Kyle yelled, tossing Pooh Bear to the floor. Before

Olivia could stop him, he ran to the door and opened it.

"Well, if it isn't the head of the household. How are you, Kyle Crawford?" The delight in her father's voice had Olivia yanking off her apron and hurrying to the door.

"Dad! I'm so glad to see you," she said, throwing her arms around her father. "Where's Mom?"

"I'm here," Edwina said from behind him, her words tentative.

"Is everything okay?" Olivia asked. Her mind raced over what could have happened to bring her parents to her door.

They'd never done it before.

She'd only seen them briefly each Christmas and Easter. Although they'd sent Kyle a birthday gift each year, they'd never accepted her invitation to celebrate.

Edwina gathered Kyle into her arms and hugged him. His gaze swerved from one grandparent to the other. "Did you bring me a present?" he asked, his expression hopeful, his thumb slipping into his mouth.

"We did, young man," Edwina said, holding him close while her eyes met Olivia's. "We came to celebrate Kyle's birthday…if you'll have us."

Olivia hesitated. The past five years that included the lonely months when she was pregnant and afraid, kept her where she stood. Ever since the day she'd told her parents about her pregnancy, she'd waited for them to show some sign of forgiveness and acceptance.

As she stood there, feelings of resentment and loss came first, followed quickly by an aching need to have a real family, a need to make Kyle's life as complete as possible.

She could let the past hold sway over the future, or she could let it go. Whatever had brought about the change in attitude didn't matter, Olivia decided; she was more than happy to have her parents here with her to celebrate Kyle's day.

"That would be so nice, Mom," she said, feeling tears prickling her lids. "Alex is at the restaurant, some sort of emergency. But he should be here any minute," she said, kissing her mother's cheek.

"That's perfect," her father said, "because we want a chance to talk to you."

"What about?"

"Let's go and sit down."

Biting her lower lip in anxiety, she led them to the living room and two large overstuffed blue-and-white-striped sofas.

"What is it? Is anything wrong? You're not sick?" Her heart pounding, she glanced from her mother to her father.

The three adults watched as Kyle raced out of the living room and into the family room.

"We're fine," her father said, once Kyle was out of earshot.

He clasped his hands; he and Edwina exchanged a quick look. "We really miss you and Kyle. We want you to know we're sorry for suggesting you give up your child for adoption, aren't we, Edwina?"

Her mother's gaze met Olivia's. "I love you. I should never have said what I said. You were forced to manage pretty much on your own, and you did. You and Alex are good parents. You did what was right for your son."

How long had she waited to hear these words? To know that her parents loved her and wanted to be part of her life. "You mean it?"

Edwina nodded. "We're so sorry for our behavior and we'd like to make amends," Edwina said.

Olivia rounded the coffee table and sat down between her parents. Wrapping her arms around both of them, she whispered, "I'm sorry, too. I really need you here with me. I've missed you so much."

And in the few minutes they embraced, Olivia finally felt at home in the house she shared with Alex. She and her parents talked to one another the way they used to, and Olivia's life began to come into focus. Her long period of isolation, of being distanced from her own history, was ending.

When Alex arrived home, he found Olivia in the kitchen making dinner and her parents happily playing with LEGO bricks as Kyle drove a huge yellow dump truck around the structure her father had built with the brightly colored pieces.

"Well, this is a nice surprise," Alex said. He kissed Olivia, a question looming in his eyes.

"Mom and Dad came to visit us and celebrate Kyle's birthday. Isn't that great?"

"It is," Alex said, going into the family room and kneeling beside Kyle.

"You've got a big fan club there, young man," he said, sending his in-laws a smile of welcome as he tousled Kyle's hair.

"Dinner will be ready in about twenty minutes. Is your mother coming over?" Olivia asked.

They'd had a big discussion two days ago about celebrating Kyle's birthday at their house rather than going to his mother's. Alex had agreed to tell her about their plan and to invite her to dinner.

"Mom can't make it," he said with a shrug of apology.

"I'm sorry to hear that," was all Olivia said.

"How's your mother doing, Alex?" her father asked, but Olivia was too busy setting the table to follow the conversation.

She sympathized with Alex, who was torn between her and his mother. But he had to choose where he belonged, had to stand up to his mother.

Nothing in life was ever easy, Olivia mused as she set the table with the Pooh dishes she'd bought on impulse.

Kyle was in a bear phase, and she'd bought him everything sold with Pooh Bear on it, from dishes to sleepers.

She'd do *anything* to see Kyle laugh, to make him happy.

Later, when they were eating cake and chuckling at her son's antics, her father said, "You don't suppose you'd like a little company for a while? Edwina says if they can put a man on the moon, I should be able to find something other than gardening to do on my vacation."

Olivia smiled at her husband, her hopes raised by the fact that her parents wanted to be with her.

"Stay as long as you like," Alex offered and Olivia felt like hugging him for his generosity.

"That's good, because we thought we might stay for a couple of weeks, just so we can get to know Kyle better," her father said.

"We're more than willing to babysit while we're here, if you need us to," Edwina added, her smile suddenly nervous.

"We'd love that Mom, we really would."

"You don't have to take care of him, simply enjoy him," Alex said.

Happiness slid through Olivia. "Thanks, honey," she murmured.

"You're welcome," Alex answered, his smile warm, his gaze suggestive. Olivia knew what that look meant. Alex wanted a baby of his own, and tonight they'd try again.

She wished she was capable of loving Alex the way he deserved. But try as she might, she couldn't feel love for him—caring, appreciation, even attraction, but not the soul-to-soul love she'd known with James.

And her guilt over that made her doubt herself. What kind of woman was she? Why couldn't she love him?

She knew only too well what the answer was.

"It'll be so much fun," she said. "Just the five of us, like we are now," she said, forcing guilty memories of the past from her mind. "Having Mom and Dad here will be terrific."

And it was. Over the next few days, Olivia's happiness was almost complete—until her mother sat down at the kitchen table one morning after Alex had gone to work and her father had taken Kyle out to the park.

"Olivia, I need to talk to you."

"What?" Olivia asked as she put a cup of coffee on the table for her mother and poured one for herself.

Edwina didn't touch her coffee. "First, did you know Grace is graduating from Hastings College next week?"

Olivia had been so consumed by her own world, she'd completely forgotten. "No, I didn't. I don't hear from Grace." Small wonder, after the way she'd snubbed her friend.

"You've never been in touch with her?"

"I didn't dare at first and now, our lives are so different." Olivia shrugged.

"Would you like to go to her graduation? She called and invited you."

"Yes," she replied after a pause. "I would like that. I have so much I want to tell her—but what would I do about Kyle?"

"We could keep him. Why don't you go? You and Grace were always close. She'd love to see you."

Like a kaleidoscope turning, memories of her high school years played in her mind. "Thanks, Mom. I'll talk it over with Alex."

"There's something else I need to tell you."

The uncertain tone of her mother's voice made Olivia uneasy. "What is it?"

The lines around Edwina's lips tightened. "We've had several calls from James."

Olivia's heart literally jumped in her chest. "Calls? He's been calling the house?"

"Yes. I told him you weren't available. He wanted to know how he could reach you. He said he knew you hadn't gone to Hastings, and that someone had said you'd studied nursing in Bangor, but he couldn't locate you. I didn't tell him anything. And how much he's managed to learn about your life, I have no idea."

"Mom, James isn't some criminal I have to hide from. Why didn't you tell me this before?"

Edwina's cool fingers touched Olivia's. "I thought about telling you, but you're married, and James has no place in your life."

Memories tore through her mind, memories of James and the first time he said he loved her. They'd been sitting in the park reading *To Kill A Mockingbird,* when he'd suddenly taken her hand in his and told her how much he loved sitting with her and reading together—how much he loved *her* and only her.

She pulled her fingers from her mother's grasp. "Mom, is this the real reason you and Dad came here?"

"No, of course not."

"Then why didn't you tell me this before?" she repeated.

"I didn't think it mattered anymore."

"Mattered? Of course it mattered! And what happened between James and me is our business. This wasn't for you to decide."

"All those months you were pregnant and hiding out here in Bar Harbor, instead of going to Hastings like you planned, while James was living the good life in Ireland. By getting you pregnant, James ruined your chances for the future you deserved. And while you were having his son, James made a few pathetic calls to the house, but what good was that to you?" She shook her head.

"Olivia, you survived alone, married a good man and made a wonderful life for your son and yourself. You're settled now, and happy. I didn't see any good reason to tell you about the phone calls."

"Mom, what did he say?"

"He wanted your number. I didn't give it to him because I don't believe he deserves to know where you are. He's hurt you so badly already. But then…this arrived special delivery."

She took a large envelope from her lap and passed it to Olivia. "He called to be sure it got here, and begged me to bring it to you." Sighing, she said, "I began to worry that I'd made a mistake about him. What if I *hadn't* insisted you move to Bar Harbor, and you'd waited at home to hear from James? I'm still not sure. Olivia, I hope you aren't too upset with me. Your father says I'm too quick to judge people, and that whatever happens, I have no right to keep this from you."

Olivia's shaking fingers clasped the envelope while her heart trembled in her chest. "From James?"

"Yes, I assume so, and if his phone calls are any indication, he wants to see you. But, honey, think about this before you open that letter. You have a husband and son, and a life that's fulfilling. Getting mixed up with James McElroy again would cause you all sorts of problems, and the scandal of an affair…you don't want that," she said disapprovingly.

Olivia stared at the envelope, her thoughts on James. "Mom, I want to be alone for a little while."

"I understand, but remember this is the man who hurt you, the man who deserted you to raise a child alone," her mother said.

OLIVIA HAD no idea how long she stared at the envelope before she opened it. All she could think about was that night at the prom, the pain and the heartache….

Finally she tore the envelope open. A note written on beautiful cream stationery slid easily into her fingers.

Dear Olivia,
I'm sending this to your parents' address as

I don't know where to find you. I can't stop thinking about the way we parted that night, and how much I want to see you. My feelings haven't changed. I love you, and just as soon as I can, I'll be back for you.

Please wait for me. Please. I don't know how else to say it, or what to do. The only plan I could come up with was that you take the airline ticket I've enclosed and meet me in London. All you have to do is call the number on the ticket and set the date.

Please come.

James.

Olivia's heart soared, air raced into her lungs and happiness filled her soul. James still loved her! James, the love of her life, wanted her to go to him.

All she'd ever wanted or needed waited for her in London.

Getting up from the table, she stumbled to her bedroom. She opened the bottom tray of her jewelry box and took out James's high school ring. Through her tears, she read the inscription *Love is Eternal.* With shaking hands, she slid the too-big ring onto her finger.

Could it be? Could it be that *their* love was eternal?

Hugging herself, she went into the bathroom and scrubbed her face with cold water until it burned.

And still the tears came.

Tears for their lost love—their once and future love. Tears for her son, who'd never known his real father.

Tears for Alex…

CHAPTER EIGHT

OLIVIA SAT STARING out into the garden, her thoughts on James. She hadn't slept for two days, not since she'd read his letter. A letter that breathed life back into all the dreams she dreamed and made all the waiting worthwhile.

James had never stopped loving her, and she still loved him. She'd almost lost hope....

What would it feel like to have his arms around her again, to know that he wanted her? A warm flush ran up her body.

And London—she'd only ever imagined going to London.

They'd spend glorious days together at some romantic hotel, talking about so many things. And at night they'd make love.

And there was Kyle. She had so much to tell James about their son.

How would James feel when he found out about Kyle? Could they build their lives together, knowing Kyle didn't understand what was going on? And how could she even *think* about taking Kyle away from Alex? Kyle meant everything to him.

How could she contemplate the idea of meeting James when she had a husband and family to consider?

"Earth to Olivia," Alex said, approaching the kitchen table with a cup of coffee in his hands.

She couldn't possibly explain why she had to go to London without Alex. She gave him a guilty glance. "Sorry," she murmured as he sat down across from her.

"What have you got there?" Alex asked, taking a sip of his coffee.

Olivia's gaze flew to the envelope she'd been clutching. Foolishly, she'd kept it with her, like a talisman. James had held this…. She tucked it into her lap. "Just a letter."

"From the college? Will you be able to take the courses you want this fall?"

She'd almost forgotten her plan to register for some business courses. After Alex had discouraged her from returning to work at the restaurant, they'd compromised by agreeing that she should look into taking courses toward her degree. "Yes," she lied, guilt forming a hard lump in her throat.

"I think it's a good idea to get started on your degree."

Her husband was offering her a chance to do

something she enjoyed. He was trying to change his attitude; in his own way, he was showing her that he valued her abilities.

How could she sit across from Alex and plan a trip to London with another man? "I'd love to get my degree someday," she said.

"Olivia, your happiness is important to me. And if going to college makes you happy, I'm all for it."

"Thanks," she whispered as her mind continued to follow its traitorous path.

"I have to go to work, but you figure it out and we'll talk tonight."

Feeling ungrateful and cowardly, Olivia watched him go out the door leading to the garage.

After Alex left, Olivia paced the floor, trying to decide what to do. Her parents had taken Kyle to the park and she was alone in the house with her memories of James—and the sense that her life was slipping out of control.

Years of being together had formed a bond between her and Alex, a bond based on Kyle and on the demands and routines of their everyday lives. But Olivia yearned for James.

What she felt for Alex was not what she felt for James. And yet…did that mean her love for James would bring her happiness?

If she told James about Kyle, James would insist on having his son in his life. She'd made a promise to herself and to Kyle that he wouldn't have to go through the agony of discovering that Alex wasn't his real father. She was determined to spare him that.

As she continued to struggle, she wished she could talk to Grace. They'd been so close. Why not call her?

Grace was probably at home with her parents, getting ready for graduation. They could talk about her plan to attend.

Before she could change her mind, she dialed the Underhills' number. As she listened to the ringing, she organized what she'd say.

She'd apologize for not keeping in touch. She'd tell Grace she wanted to see her, take her up on her offer to attend the graduation. They'd meet for lunch.

Once they were together, she'd talk to Grace about James, about her feelings for him. And when Grace learned that she was married with a child—if she didn't already know—she'd be horrified that Olivia would even consider abandoning her marriage.

What if Grace was angry and hostile with her, or worse, wouldn't talk to her? Her disapproval would end any chance of renewing their friendship.

And what if Olivia let it slip that Kyle was James's son? What would Grace do? Grace had grown up around the McElroy family; she'd feel obligated to tell them about Kyle.

If Grace *did* tell them, and the McElroys decided to claim him, Alex would be crushed, and Olivia would face the battle of trying to keep her son from the clutches of a powerful family.

The answering machine came on, inviting her to leave a message.

If she went to Grace's graduation, she'd end up confiding in Grace things that were better left unsaid. There was too much at stake, too many people who'd be devastated if she shared her secret.

She put the phone down.

OLIVIA MANAGED to get through the rest of the day without doing what she wanted to do more than anything in the world. She hadn't called the number James had put in his letter.

"We had a lot of fun," Edwina gushed, sliding the patio door shut behind her. "Your father and Kyle are out in the backyard, playing catch. Your father has dreams of getting Kyle into baseball, and did you know your son wants a dog?"

Olivia wrenched her thoughts away from James. "No, I didn't, but we could think about it," she said as her mother made coffee.

She couldn't remember when she'd enjoyed

being with her mother like this. Maybe it was the fact that they were both mothers now, or maybe it was simply time for them to become friends. "I'm so glad you and Dad are here, Mom."

"We're glad, too. Your father was the one who insisted we come and try to make amends, and at first I wasn't convinced…but he was right. You're a very forgiving person, Olivia," she said, smoothing the hair from Olivia's brow.

At her mother's touch, she felt a serenity, a sense of caring and approval. "Mom, sit down. I need your advice. I'm not sure what I should do."

"Of course, honey." Her mother pulled out a chair and sat down.

Olivia told her about James and what he wanted.

"You're not going, are you?" her mother asked, disbelief knitting her brows.

"Mom, I've always loved James. Things haven't turned out the way we planned. But I have a right to know if they still could, don't I?"

"A *right?* I'm not sure about that. I know you have a responsibility to Kyle. And to the man you married."

"What are you saying?"

"I can't begin to imagine why you'd consider going to London to meet a man who abandoned you when you needed him most."

"But Mom, he didn't know I was pregnant! And

I had no one who was willing to help me find him, to tell him he was going to be a father."

"Has it occurred to you that maybe James hasn't been in touch because he doesn't *want* to be?"

Her mother had just put Olivia's worst fear into words. But surely whatever had kept him in Ireland all these years didn't involve her. "James didn't have any say about going to Ireland," she argued.

She had her ticket to London as proof that he still cared. "And if you didn't want me to see James again, why did you bring me this letter?"

Edwina sighed heavily. "Because I made a mistake five years ago by not supporting your choice of waiting for James. If I had, you would've been free to marry James now and make a life with him. But with your marriage to Alex… Well, I'd hoped you'd be able to answer James's letter without yearning for what might have been."

"Mom, what if I *do* want to make a life with James? We've never stopped loving each other—"

"Don't let Alex hear you say that! The man loves you."

"Mom, Alex and I have…an arrangement."

"That may have been true in the beginning, but not now. Your father and I have both noticed how Alex looks at you. And if your head wasn't in the clouds over James, you'd see it, too."

"You talked to Dad about this?"

"Of course. We're both concerned about James and his determination to get in touch with you. And we're both worried that the past you had with him could turn you away from your life with Alex. If you want my opinion, what you feel for James is infatuation, some fantasy about how you're destined to be together. It's not the love of a mature man and a woman."

Olivia gaped at her mother. "How can you say that?"

"Because I've been where you are. I remember how it feels to fall madly in love for the first time. But that's all it is, a first-time love, not something that'll last. Don't destroy what you have for a second chance at some teenage crush."

"Mom, it's the seventies. People get divorced all the time."

"Smart women don't. Not when the man they're married to loves them. Don't you see how lucky you are to have a wonderful son and a man like Alex?"

"Yes, I'm lucky, but that doesn't mean I'm happy."

"You won't let yourself be happy. Happiness comes from doing what's best for those you love."

"I've always loved James," she said stubbornly.

"Are you willing to risk your son's happiness? If you take Kyle from the only father he's ever known, what then? What kind of happiness is that for a little boy who didn't do anything but love his parents?"

They both turned at the sound of the door.

"I'm home," Alex said, striding toward them a moment later. "Where's Kyle?"

Guilt shrouded Olivia's thoughts as she saw the way Alex looked at her, the way his smile waited for hers. And in that instant, she felt a need to protect him from pain and sadness. He'd been her lifeline these past years, and she owed him her loyalty.

He'd told her in so many ways that he wanted their marriage to work, and he'd changed his attitude about her needing to have a life outside their home.

His mother was a major obstacle to their happiness, but Alex had begun to make an effort to keep her out of their lives. James, however, hadn't been able to put her feelings ahead of his father's demands.

"Waiting for you to come home," Olivia said, returning her husband's smile.

"Kyle's out back, learning how to catch a ball," her mother said, her eyes meeting Olivia's.

"Then I'll go join the men." Alex smiled again, sliding the patio door open and going out into the backyard.

"Do what's right, Olivia. And do it now," her mother warned.

Olivia wished she could go back to the week before, to Kyle's fourth birthday, when life had been less confusing.

After her mother went upstairs, Olivia stood at the sliding glass doors, watching her son. The smile on Kyle's face, and his delight when he caught the ball Alex threw him, so gently, made her heart pound with joy.

Turning away from the door, she went to the desk in the den and took out the envelope James had sent her. Hurriedly, she emptied the contents into a new envelope, scribbled James's return address on the front and sealed it. Crossing the room, she picked up her purse and placed the envelope inside.

IF ONLY SHE hadn't taken her mother's advice that day, Olivia mused as she glanced around the hospital waiting room. She would have saved everyone—including Alex—so much unhappiness. She remembered how easily she'd given in to Edwina's urging.

Her mother now sat beside Grace; her parents had arrived this morning. Her dad had gone down to the lobby to look for a paper.

"When are we going to be allowed to see James?" Grace demanded.

"*You* will not be allowed to see him, I've told you that," Olivia said, gritting her teeth.

"I don't understand why not," Grace argued, her face tight with disapproval.

"We've been through that. You know the rules."

"Yes, just his family. But without me, you might never have been his wife. I'm going to go and have a cigarette. If they haven't let you in by the time I get back, I'm going to lodge a complaint."

"Don't do that," Edwina said, her voice firm. "You're only going to make things more difficult for Olivia and James. The sooner you recognize that, the better off we'll be."

Grace glared at Edwina, but said nothing.

Grace strode out of the waiting room in a huff. "Thanks, Mom. I don't know what I'm going to do with her, but one more outburst like that, and she's out of here."

"Grace is spoiled. She grew up getting her own way. That's how she thinks. You leave her to me. I'll talk some sense into her."

The nurse entered the room. "Mrs. McElroy? You can visit Mr. McElroy now."

Olivia leaped out of the chair. "Oh, thank you! How's he doing?" she asked breathlessly, as she and the nurse moved toward the Intensive Care.

"He's holding his own. We're observing him carefully, and he seems to be responding well," the nurse said, her eyes sympathetic.

Stepping quietly into his room, Olivia gazed

down at James, lying so still in the narrow bed. The tube in his throat was gone, and the nurse had told her she could visit for a longer period. "James, darling, I'm here," she whispered close to his ear.

The heart monitor pinged faster. James opened his eyes.

"You're awake," she said, taking his hand in hers, willing him her strength. His eyes fluttered closed.

He gave her fingers a feeble squeeze.

"I've been waiting for you to wake up, sleepy-head," she said, her spirits rising despite the confusion she saw on his face. "You're going to be fine. You'll be back tending your garden before you know it." Olivia smiled encouragingly.

"Missed you," James whispered, over an odd gurgling sound in his throat. He tried to turn toward her, but an array of tubes and wires effectively restrained him.

"Me, too, darling."

"Kyle? Here?"

"No, not yet, but I'm sure he'll be here soon. Don't worry about anything. Just get better," she said, her throat tightening against the panic she suddenly felt.

Dr. Crealock had said that James wasn't doing quite as well as he'd hoped, and although the doctor had been supportive, Olivia recognized just how precarious things were with her husband.

"Stay with me," James said, his breathing labored. She could see the struggle in his eyes as a cough tore from his throat.

There was so much that still had to be said between them, but fear of upsetting him held her back. "I'll stay with you, always."

"Olivia, be happy, whatever happens. Even if this doesn't turn out the way we—" A spasm of coughing racked him, and Olivia's hands shook in his.

"Please don't talk," she said urgently. "It's too hard on you."

Olivia studied the rapid rise and fall of his chest and heard the rattling sound of his breathing. "I'm going to call the nurse."

"No, stay with me. Please…"

She did.

THROUGH THE haze of medication, James saw the worry in Olivia's eyes, the strange room behind her, and tried once again to sort out his thoughts. Beneath his confusion lay a horrible fear that he might die. And Olivia would be alone once more.

The past and the present seemed to be all mixed-up in his mind. He'd been reliving a memory…. He was in Dublin when he'd faced the crushing truth—his life with Olivia would never be….

After James had sent her the ticket at her parents' address, he'd called to be sure it had arrived.

Edwina had agreed to get the ticket to Olivia, but promised nothing more. The waiting was sheer agony, but he'd kept believing Olivia would come.

He had so many dreams of what it would be like when she stepped off the plane in London. With Uncle Seamus's help, he'd located the perfect hotel in downtown London and had ordered a tourist guide to London's many attractions.

The guidebook arrived in the mail the same day her ticket did.

At first, he couldn't guess what the plain brown envelope contained. The postmark was smudged but the address was written by Olivia; he'd recognize her penmanship anywhere. The tightness in his chest was nearly unbearable as he pulled the ticket out. He'd searched the envelope three times for a note from Olivia, anything to tell him why she'd returned the ticket.

For weeks, he couldn't concentrate on his work, overwhelmed by a profound sense of loss. Olivia didn't want to see him. He'd tried to make contact with her, convince her to meet him, without success. What reason did she have for not seeing him? Was she married? No, she couldn't be; her mother would have told him during the first call he'd made to her house, or one of his friends would've let him know.

He had to consider the very real possibility that Olivia didn't love him anymore, that the life she was leading was more important to her than a reunion with him. And yet, he couldn't blame her. He'd let fear of his father and his indecision rob him of the woman he loved.

Finally, one day, when he'd confessed to his uncle what had happened, Seamus insisted he go home to find Olivia.

With his uncle's blessing, he called his father from his office. He'd called home infrequently during the past years and the reception was always the same—cool. Unfriendly. Occasionally he got his mother, who talked about how much she missed him, and asked when he was coming home.

As childish as it sounded, he was more at ease calling his father from work, perhaps because it put him on an equal footing with the man who could still intimidate him. His father's private line rang five times before he answered.

"Hi, Dad, it's James."

"Good morning, son. How's your day? Nearly half over, I assume," his father said, noting the five-hour time difference.

"Everything's fine. I talked to Mom on Sunday and she said she's busy with Easter preparations at the church."

"That's your mother. Now what can I do for you?"

James took a deep breath. "Dad, I'm sure Uncle Seamus has told you about my work here, how well I'm doing."

"He has. He's very pleased to have you with him."

"Well, Dad, you remember when you and I talked the night I left?"

"I remember."

"And I asked if you'd consider letting me come back and work for you once I had some experience over here."

"I remember," his father said again, his voice flat.

From past experience, James knew that whenever his father spoke in that tone, he wasn't happy. The old James, the one who'd always done his father's bidding, wouldn't have taken the conversation any further for fear of antagonizing him.

But things had changed with the return of the ticket. If he didn't take a stand with his father where Olivia was concerned, he'd never see her again, never have another chance.

He *had* to go home. "I was wondering if you'd let me work for you in Frampton. I've learned a lot about business over the past few years." He knew he sounded too eager—almost desperate. "I could act as your assistant, maybe even take over while you and Mom go on vacation. With me there, you'd be able to relax and enjoy some time away from the office."

There was a long silence. Just as James was about to hang up and call back, his father said, "No one, and especially not my son, is going to take this job from me until I'm ready to go. Besides, you don't have the maturity to do it. You left here a naive, inexperienced young man. I sent you to your uncle so you could grow up a little, get a life going for yourself, away from the crowd you were hanging out with at school."

Resentment curled slowly through him. "Yes," he said, his voice growing stronger. "I may have been irresponsible back then, but I'm not anymore."

"Don't raise your voice to me," his father said abruptly, which had always been his way of dismissing his children's opinions.

But this time James refused to be dismissed. He lowered his voice. "I'm sorry, Dad. I didn't realize I was raising my voice. I called to tell you I'm coming home."

Silence again. "What have you done about getting a life for yourself over there in Dublin?" his father finally asked. "Do you have friends?"

"Dad, it's hard to make friends when you work such long hours. And that's what I've been doing— working hard so I can prove myself to you."

"Well, you've proven you can do the job. Now go out and have some fun. Have you met any eligible women?"

Seamus had dutifully invited a dozen women to dinner over the five years James had been here, but none of them interested him. "Yes, I've met several nice women, but—"

"But what? Are you still pining over that Banks girl?"

"Dad, listen to me! I'm coming home," he said, forcing the words out against the thudding of his heart.

"Son, home is where your work is. Home is where you make it. I had to leave Ireland, leave everything familiar in my life, and come here to the States. I wanted to go back, but my father wouldn't hear of it. I had to obey my father—and you do, too."

During his years here in Dublin, he'd lived with the hope that Thomas McElroy would come to accept him for the man he'd become. But that acceptance would never be his.

"Dad, the world's changed. I respect you, and you have to respect me. I'm a man now, and I make my own decisions. I've done everything you asked. I didn't go to college and I gave up my friends, all so I could be the son you wanted. Now I'm coming home, and you can't stop me."

"My warning still stands. You come home and Banks loses his job."

Silence radiated from the phone, followed by a click and the buzz of a disconnected line.

"I NEVER spoke to my father after that day."

"What, honey? What are you talking about?" Olivia asked.

He looked up into Olivia's eyes, and his pulse pounded in his head as he realized that somehow she was beside him. "You're here?"

"Yes, darling, I'm here."

Her smile lifted the chill from the room. "Is everything all right?" he asked.

"James, everything's fine. Were you dreaming?"

"Maybe…I was just remembering things that happened years ago. My mind must be wandering."

"Don't worry, dear. You're getting better."

James wasn't sure exactly where he was. He glanced around.

"You're in the hospital, and your surgery is over. I'm going to stay with you. I promise."

The flow of air through the tube in his nose made him want to sneeze. "It's all the memories…"

"What sort of memories?"

Feeling suddenly very tired, he whispered, "Not important. Talk to me. Tell me what you remember."

"Let me think. There are so many things. We've been through so much, you and me."

"Do you remember that day at the cottage?" he asked, fighting to keep his voice steady.

"Yes," she said. "How could I ever forget? How helpless I felt, and how little chance we had."

"The worst day of my life," he murmured, a sad smile laying claim to his haggard features.

CHAPTER NINE

NINETEEN YEARS after leaving home, James came back to bury his father. As he and Julia, along with their mother, stood in front of his father's casket, it didn't seem possible that he'd feared the old man the way he did.

So many of the mourners had praised Tom McElroy's generosity and enthusiasm. James was thirty-seven years old and he'd never seen that side of the man who'd fathered him.

In those first lonely years he'd spent under his uncle's supervision in Ireland, he'd often wondered what it might've been like to have a normal, caring relationship with his father. But after that last call with his father, he'd given up hope of ever having any real rapport with Tom McElroy.

Still, a part of him had always clung to the idea that someday he'd do something that would please his father, something that would let him into his father's heart.

And now it was too late.

After that final call about coming home, he'd booked his flight for Boston, determined to find Olivia, but his plan ended with a message from Uncle Seamus's housekeeper. His uncle had seen the doctor because of a persistent cough and had just been told he had lung cancer.

In that moment of fear and dread, James had known that he couldn't possibly leave his uncle to the care of strangers.

He gave up his townhouse and moved into his uncle's house. From that day on, he didn't leave the dying man's side except to go to the office when it was absolutely necessary. He'd set up a home office so he could look after the company's management as much as possible from the house.

He wanted Seamus to know that everything was under control, that all he had to do was concentrate on getting better.

They were conspirators in the belief that if they denied his illness and its inevitable outcome it would somehow go away.

As the months moved slowly forward, James saw the decay transform his uncle's body into a hollow frame, held together by bones drawn to the surface of his discolored skin. Changes he was helpless to stop.

And for the first time in his life, he prayed with all his heart and soul. But his prayers ended two years later when his uncle died. Seamus McElroy had been his father in every way but birth. He would never forget him.

The day Seamus died, James called his parents to tell them. His mother explained that his father wouldn't be coming to the funeral, nor would she. His father had suffered a heart attack and was in the hospital.

He offered to come home, but his parents seemed indifferent. Left alone to mourn the loss of his uncle, James worked long hours, making Laurel Industries one of the most successful companies in Ireland.

He'd abandoned any thought of searching for Olivia. Wherever her life had taken her, he assumed she was happy with it. As for James, he'd grown accustomed to a feeling of emptiness, which over the years became simply a part of who he was.

During those years, he met a beautiful woman whose career as a sculptor was the focus of her life. They'd had a wonderful affair and he'd nearly married her. But Cynthia Maddox had been wiser than he. She'd seen something in him that told her that he wasn't really free to marry her. He held fast to his denial without exploring the possibility that Cynthia was right.

In the meanwhile, Julia came to Dublin to visit and to scold him about his monastic existence.

And he routinely called to inquire about his father. Tom went back to work the next year, and everything seemed to be fine.

When the call came that he'd had another heart attack, James made arrangements to fly home. Before he could get there, his father took a turn for the worse and died.

Feeling somehow detached from the funeral, he watched in the frigid January air as they lowered his father into the cold ground. His mother stood beside him, her shoulders straight, her eyes now clear and unclouded by tears.

"Are you all right?" he asked his mother, studying her for any sign of emotion other than stoic calm.

"Your father would want us to be strong, to show what the McElroy name stood for." She continued to stare at his father's grave.

James had never known his mother to cry—until the day he came home for his father's funeral. She'd been waiting for him at the house, her color a ghastly shade of gray. Yet not a strand of her platinum hair had escaped the effects of the hair spray she always used.

"Mom, is there anything else I can do for you?" he asked softly, afraid that standing so long in the cold could make her ill.

"You already did all the damage you could

when you defied your father. But you got your way, didn't you?"

"What are you saying?"

"Your call really upset your father."

"Mom, that was years ago!"

"You defied him," she said again, her face expressionless. "And all because you wanted to run with that Banks girl and ruin your life."

"Mom, don't talk about Olivia that way!"

His mother looked up at him, her gaze rigid. "You're still involved with her. I can see it in your eyes."

How little his mother knew about his life. He'd lost Olivia, but he no longer wanted to blame anyone. Olivia belonged in the past.

Julia slid her hand into his. "Don't let Mom get to you," she whispered.

He put his arm around his sister's shoulders and stepped back to let people pay their respects to his mother. "I'm glad you're here," he said in a low voice.

"Me, too. And I'll be glad to get back to New York. You're going to come and visit now that you're home, I hope."

"Wouldn't miss the chance. We have so much to catch up on. Oh, by the way, I had a call from Sean Cotter, telling me how much he appreciated your help in getting his daughter's life straightened out. It must feel good to see a patient get better," he said, proud that his little sister had made a success of her life despite their father's interference. He was also glad to learn that she'd reconciled with him before he died.

"It is. I love being a psychologist, especially when I see one of my patients show improvement like Sean's daughter did. Did I ever tell you I had a giant crush on Sean when I was in grade school?"

"No, you didn't. Why didn't you tell me?"

"Your love life wasn't the only reason I helped you and Olivia keep your secret. I wanted Sean to notice me."

"Really?" he asked, remembering the excitement of those lost times. "I never suspected…. Did Sean know?"

"No, I don't think so, but that didn't stop me from dreaming about Sean. Needless to say, I was more than happy to counsel his daughter, for old times' sake." Julia squinted up at him and smiled. "Besides, she's a good person who simply needed to work through some issues. Not unlike the rest of us, I might add."

James glanced at his sister, pleased that she was contented with her life. "Does that smile have anything to do with the guy who drove you up here for the service?"

"It does. John couldn't stay, but I'll see him on the weekend."

"I'm glad for you."

"And what about you? Did you ever get in touch with Olivia?"

"Yes and no. It's complicated."

"I understand. We can't talk here, but we will when you come to New York. Promise?"

"I promise."

"Just in case one of your far-flung business interests should prevent you from coming to see me, I want to say just one thing."

"And that would be?"

"If you still love Olivia, fight for her. I nearly lost John until I realized he's everything I want and need in this world."

"Thanks," he whispered, looking over her head at the mourners moving away from the graveside.

Julia brushed his cheek with a kiss. "I've got to go and talk to a classmate of mine over there, but I'll be back. Remember what I said."

He was about to take his mother's arm and guide her to the car when Grace Underhill appeared beside him. "How are you doing?" she asked, giving him a hug.

He hugged her back. "All right, I guess," he said, relieved to have someone other than his mother to talk to. Grace could be counted on to chat about frivolous things, a distraction he needed at the moment.

She edged closer, her musky perfume filling his nostrils.

There was something so needy about Grace, and always had been from the first day he'd met her in grade school. Their families socialized together, which made a friendship between them almost inevitable.

He'd spent many a day walking Grace home from school, under strict orders from his mother to treat her with care and respect. They'd been friends, but that was all it would ever be for him. Grace didn't have the drive and enthusiasm for life that attracted him. Yet, seeing Grace lightened his otherwise dark, introspective mood.

"How long are you in town?" she asked.

"Another ten days, and then I have to get back to Ireland."

"Want to go to lunch next week? We could do a little catching up."

He met Grace's inquiring gaze. She was a beautiful woman by anyone's standards. "Sure, why not?"

"It's been ages since I've seen you," Grace smiled into his face, her lips slightly parted, her eyes hinting at more.

"Lunch it is, then," he said. With a backward

wave Grace strolled away from the graveyard, her hips swaying, her shoulders straight under her black silk suit that accentuated every curve.

"Don't become another notch on that woman's belt," Julia admonished a moment later. "I saw her making a beeline for you."

"Grace isn't all that bad."

"Ask her ex. Our darling Grace convinced him not to have a prenuptial agreement, then took him for over two million."

"You're kidding."

"Wish I were…I never liked that woman. She always seems to have an agenda. I wonder what she wants from you, my handsome, rich, single brother? Hmm?"

He raised an eyebrow. "According to my friends, I'm immune to beautiful women."

"Yeah, right," Julia scoffed, with a light punch to her brother's arm.

"How much harm can she do over lunch?"

"If you want my advice, I'd say batten down your wallet."

THE NEXT WEEK, when James sat down across from Grace at one of the best tables in Mario's Ristorante, he recognized the signs. She was on a mission that involved him.

He'd entertained the idea of canceling the date,

but what the hell else did he have to do? He'd sold McElroy Manufacturing's operations in Frampton, a subsidiary of Laurel Industries, to a consortium in South Carolina for a good price. And in a declining textile industry, that was a feat.

He'd been surprised to learn that his father's name had a certain cachet, which made the sale much easier than he'd expected. The proceeds of the sale of McElroy Manufacturing became part of the assets of Laurel Industries, its parent company. Because his uncle had made him beneficiary of his stock in Laurel, James now held controlling interest in a very large company. His father's will had made a modest provision for him while his mother and sister inherited the bulk of the estate.

"I'm afraid my life is nothing but business these days," he said, answering Grace's inquiry about what he did with his evenings.

She grinned over the rim of her glass. "That's not what I've heard. I heard you were dating a well-known artist in Dublin, a very upscale and worldly artist at that. I heard you might be proposing to her."

"All rumors," he said dismissively, wondering just how Grace knew about his off-again, on-again affair with Cynthia.

"I love rumors. Want to tell me about her?" she asked, giving him a coquettish smile.

"There's not much to tell. Cynthia's a wonderful woman and a great artist. I have several of her sculptures."

"Is that all?"

He shrugged, smiled and tried to come up with a different topic of conversation. "Sorry to disappoint you."

"Come on. I don't believe this. No wedding bells in your future?"

He and Cynthia still saw each other—as friends. Because she'd been so supportive when his uncle was ill, they'd developed a special bond.

"What's new with you?" he asked, jumping on the only subject that came to mind. "Anyone in your life?"

"I wish." Grace stirred her drink, her lacquered nails flashing a shiny red. "I've been busy getting my interior design company up and running. That's been fun, but far too much work."

"That's how it goes when you own your own business."

"So it seems." Grace smoothed the napkin under her martini glass. "Then there were my mother's health issues. I spent all of last spring here, trying to organize home care for her. I was glad to get back to my condo in New York," Grace said, a glum expression on her carefully made-up face.

He nodded noncommittally.

Grace surveyed her polished fingernails. "By the way, I saw Edwina Banks when I was home with Mom. She's certainly aged since the last time I saw her, although it's been years, I have to admit. We chatted, and I asked about Olivia."

A hard lump formed in his chest. "Olivia?"

"Yeah, I haven't heard a word from her since the day she left. I invited her to my graduation, but she didn't call me back. So I didn't see much point in contacting her, and besides I didn't know how to reach her." Grace shook her head. "Edwina didn't have much to say except that Olivia married some man by the name of Alex Crawford and is living in Bar Harbor."

A flood of feelings—longing, love and need— roared through James, twisting his heart into a searing knot of pain.

He'd told himself over and over that she was someone he'd once loved.

He'd told himself that time had erased her from his life.

He'd told himself a lie.

"Did you call her?" he asked over his racing heart and the rush of yearning that claimed him. "After you talked to her mother?"

"I thought about it, but in the end I didn't. I'm still hurt about the way she snubbed me after you dropped her. I always wondered if she blamed me for your disappearance."

"What? Why would she blame you?" James asked—anything to keep Grace's mind on something other than him.

All he wanted to do was slip away to someplace quiet while he dealt with the pain of knowing that Olivia was married to someone else. Had she rejected his offer of a trip to London because of that?

Grace's smile was shaky as she bent her head to meet his gaze. "Are you all right, James?"

"Why do you ask?" he countered.

Grace finished her martini and waved the waiter over. "You just looked a little odd for a minute there."

He planted a smile on his face. "Back to what you said. Why would Olivia blame you for anything?"

"Just a feeling. Because of what your father did when he found out about Olivia."

"How do you know so much about what happened if you haven't talked to Olivia?"

"Your mother, who else? She and I talked after you went to Ireland, and I've had Christmas cards from her every year since you moved. She's been keeping me up to date on what's going on in your life. Do you suppose she has an ulterior motive?" Grace asked coyly.

"Well, I'll be damned," James said, anger rising in him. Why would his mother do that? He'd told her more than once that he wasn't interested in Grace, and still she persisted.

Maybe his mother was more involved in what had occurred that night at the prom than he realized. Maybe it wasn't just his father who thought Olivia was unsuitable. Had he been a naive, compliant son to both parents while they wreaked havoc on his emotional life? James gave a harsh laugh.

"What's so funny?"

"Not a thing."

Grace tapped her nails on the shiny surface of the table. "You know, I sensed that Edwina was hiding something. She seemed evasive when I asked if Olivia was happy. She did tell me that the guy Olivia married is a very successful business-man in Bar Harbor."

"I'm glad for her." Pain, mingled with regret, forced the words from his lips.

"Are you *sure?*" Grace asked, her eyes sweeping his face.

He couldn't tell her how he really felt; he couldn't tell anyone. It was his secret. He'd left Olivia to make a life for herself, and she had. Now it was up to him to live with it. "Olivia deserves to be happy," he muttered, "and it sounds like she is."

"Olivia deserved to go to college, like she planned. She was so good in school. I'll never understand what changed her mind about going to Hastings," Grace said with a lift of her thin, perfectly tanned shoulders.

A long-buried dream stirred in him. Olivia had been the one person in his life who'd believed in him unconditionally. What he wouldn't give to see her again. He needed to share his grief about Seamus with her, and hear her comforting words about the uncle he'd loved. He wanted to tell her he'd planned to come home and find her when his uncle had been diagnosed with cancer.

For the first time he clearly saw what he needed to do—had needed to do all along. His sharp intake of breath drew a quick response from Grace.

"Hey, what's up?" she asked. "You can tell me."

He met her inquiring glance head-on. "Not at the moment. I have to make a phone call. Will you excuse me?"

"Sure." Sipping her third martini, Grace threw him a quizzical look.

As he left the table he could feel her intense scrutiny. He had no intention of telling her a thing. He was going to contact Olivia and find out for certain whether she was happy. If she had a good life that didn't include him, he'd make himself forget her.

Besides, after all the years he'd waited and all their dreams and plans, he owed it to himself to see her one last time.

Olivia Crawford would be easy to locate now that he knew she lived in Bar Harbor. The difficult part would be actually seeing her again.

CHAPTER TEN

Two weeks later

OLIVIA HAD JUST finished her first assignment for her Business Management course when the phone rang. It was only the third week of January, but the sudden chill had affected everything, including the heating system at the restaurant. Anxious to hear from her husband, Olivia was quick to pick up the phone. "Hi," she said, expecting to hear Alex telling her he'd be late getting home.

"Is this Olivia Banks?" a man's voice asked.

No one had called her by her maiden name in years. "Yes. Who's calling?"

"It's Sean Cotter from high school. Do you remember me?"

Sean Cotter. *Oh, God. James's best friend.* "Yes, I do. How are you?" she asked, holding her breath.

"I'm great. I'm in Bar Harbor and I decided I'd

look you up. I only heard a little while ago that you lived here, or I would've called sooner. I'm often in Bar Harbor on business."

"That's nice." Olivia couldn't think of what else to say. No one from home had contacted her since she'd come here, and now that someone had, she wasn't sure what to do.

"I was wondering if we might get together for coffee," he said.

It would be so nice to see some of the people she'd grown up with, to reconnect with the past, especially since she'd missed Grace's graduation. "I'd love to."

They agreed to get together for coffee at Crawford's. Olivia was working at the restaurant one day a week while the part-time accountant Alex had hired was on maternity leave.

Olivia had every intention of remaining part of the staff and it was with quiet pride that she welcomed Sean. "This is our restaurant."

"To think of all the meals I've eaten here, and never once did I run into you," Sean said, sliding into the booth across from her.

"Thanks. Alex has other business interests, but I love this restaurant."

"And it shows." Sean stared at her. "I don't suppose you've heard from James since he came back?"

"He's back?" She steadied the coffee cup in her hands letting the words sink in.

"Yes, his father died and James came home for the funeral and to settle his estate."

"I…didn't know." She'd stopped checking the Boston papers for news of him or his family a couple of years after she'd returned the ticket. It seemed pointless to continue, since James had made no further attempt to contact her.

"I saw him a couple of weeks ago, when I went to his dad's funeral. He's getting ready to go back to Ireland."

A strange ache started beneath her ribs. Memories of evenings spent driving around town in James's red Mustang—the windows down, the breeze cooling her skin, his hand holding hers—floated to the surface. Those were such carefree days, full of pleasure and excitement, when nothing mattered except spending every available hour with each other.

Were those memories happy ones for him? Or was his world made up of more sophisticated pleasures? "How was he?" she murmured.

"He's doing well, despite everything going on in his life. Grace was at the funeral, as well. Do you see her much?"

Envy nibbled at her. "No, I haven't seen Grace in years. I've been out of touch with everyone."

She met Sean's eyes and saw the sympathy in them.

"I'm glad to hear he's doing okay," she said, her glance shifting away from his. She tried desperately to hide the loneliness tearing through her, coupled with guilt about Kyle and her decision not to tell James about his son.

Impulsively, Sean reached for her hand. "I know how much you cared for James. And how much he cared for you."

She smiled to cover her awkwardness. "Thanks for saying that. I really appreciate it."

Sean tightened his grip. "I'm here because James would like to see you. He doesn't want to upset you. He knows you're married."

But did he know about Kyle?

She looked at Sean in confusion, then slid her hands into her lap and offered a silent prayer that he didn't. "I don't understand. Why did he send you instead of coming himself?"

"All I can tell you is that James wants to see you—if you want to see him. He knows it's been a long time, and that you may prefer not to see him. He just thought that if he wasn't the one to ask, you'd feel free to refuse."

James wants to see you. How long had she waited to hear those words?

All those nights after she'd returned the ticket,

when she lay awake trying to make herself believe she didn't care about James. Those moments during the day when she'd catch herself remembering and force the memory back. And now Sean sat across from her, offering her the opportunity to put those memories to rest.

Deep down, Olivia had harbored a dream that someday James would come back to reclaim her and Kyle. Was that dream about to become reality?

She needed to know how he felt about her, if there was any hope that his love for her was still alive. And if he did still love her, what would she do? She loved *him,* a love she'd denied for the good of her son.

Kyle would graduate from high school soon and leave home for university. She was free to follow her own dreams, wasn't she?

"I'm not sure what would be gained by talking to him. We haven't spoken in almost twenty years."

Sean gave a sigh of resignation. "Look, I'm the one who volunteered to come here and see you. I want my friend to be happy, and he's not. He hasn't been ever since he went to Ireland."

James had been unhappy…since he'd gone to Ireland. Since he'd had to walk out of her life. It all seemed so clear now. James had gone to satisfy his father's demands and to protect her parents' livelihood. He'd gone to a life where he had no friends, to a job he probably didn't like…to make the best of a bad situation. And while they were apart, he'd been trying to come back to her…first the phone calls and then the ticket, and now he was here waiting for word that she wanted to meet him.

"If I could change that night at the prom, if James had had a choice, how different our lives would be today," she said.

"Is that a no?" Sean asked, his expression crestfallen.

When had life gotten so complicated? She loved James; she always would. But maybe, as her mother said, it was just a dream now.

Still…wasn't everyone entitled to dream? She closed her eyes, remembering the night she'd been with James, the way he'd made love to her. And the child of that love, who'd become the focus of her life.

"When does he want to meet?"

Sean brightened. "That's up to you. He can come here, if you'd like."

She shook her head.

"Or you can meet him at my family's cottage just south of Bar Harbor. We keep it open year-round, and it's on a bluff overlooking the ocean, very cozy and private. I'll write down the directions."

Could she go behind Alex's back, keep this kind of secret from the man who shared her bed? And what did it say about her feelings for Alex?

She already knew the answer to that.

She'd grown to like Alex, to respect him. Yet never once had she felt for him what she felt for James. If there was some way to get over this yearning for another man, to finally be at peace with her life, it would be worth the lie that would allow her to meet James. Maybe then she could offer Alex more than mere affection and the companionship of friends.

"Tell James I'll meet him."

TWO DAYS LATER, on the drive to Sean's cottage, Olivia listened to a radio reporter talking about the space shuttle *Challenger*. Concentrating on what was going on with the crew kept her mind off what was about to happen in her life.

Olivia pulled in behind a black Mercedes in the driveway of the cottage Sean had directed her to. Her hands shook as she turned off the car. She'd been awake all night, fighting the urge to renege on her agreement to meet James today.

It hadn't been necessary to lie to Alex about where she was going this morning because he'd left on business early the previous day. That didn't ease the guilt she'd wrestled with during the endless night.

Hurting Alex was wrong and against everything

she believed in as a mother and a wife. Yet she'd made plans to meet James anyway.

For all her worrying and wishing, the two days since she'd talked to Sean had been infused with a strange happiness. Even Alex's mother, Caroline, had noticed how excited she was.

She tucked her hair behind her ear, and ran her hands along the edge of the fur-lined hood of her brown suede jacket. Checking her lipstick in the mirror, Olivia eased out of the seat and started along the snow-packed driveway, her palms sweating.

And suddenly he was there, standing in the entrance to the cottage. "James." She breathed his name, afraid he might disappear.

"Olivia." He took her hand, his eyes searching her face.

"You're here," she whispered.

Afraid to touch him, she pulled her hand away and edged past him into the cottage. Light shimmered on polished wood in the main room, and an off-season mustiness hung in the cool air.

She made her way to a long sofa in the middle of the room in front of a huge stone fireplace. James followed her, sitting at the opposite end.

"Did you have any trouble finding the cottage?" he asked politely.

"No, it was easy." Now that she was here with him, she couldn't think of anything to say.

"I'm glad," he said, his hands resting in his lap.

His gaze met hers and a peculiar lethargy weighted her limbs. Content to simply sit beside him, she let her gaze travel over him, noting the changes the intervening years had made.

His shoulders were just as wide as she remembered. The sideburns he once wore with pride were gone, and there was a hint of gray at his temples. He still had the longest eyelashes she'd ever seen. And she could never forget the way his mouth tilted up at the edges and the way light seemed trapped in his eyes as they held hers. He still had the power to make her feel as though she was the only woman on earth.

"I'm sorry to hear about your father."

His eyes slid away from hers. "Thank you. I've been helping my mother settle his affairs."

"That's good." She wanted to touch his cheek, to run her fingers through the gray in his hair.

"And how about you? How are your parents?"

"Fine. They keep busy." If only she dared take his hand. Were they going to sit like this forever?

"Do you see them often?"

"Yeah, they still live in the same house."

He angled his body closer to hers, his heat mingling with hers. Despite the cool air of the cottage, she felt his glance like a warm breeze on a summer day. She sat perfectly still, basking in his attention. "Do you like Ireland?"

"Yes, it's lovely."

"I've been reading about it. The area around Dublin sounds wonderful, really wonderful. Do you live right in the city?"

"Yes, I have a town house with a garden on the southeast side of Dublin."

"Near Lansdowne Road?"

"Not far from there. You really have been reading up on Dublin," he said.

He looked at the ceiling and then back at her, an anxious smile making the corners of his mouth twitch. Like the James she remembered. But uncertainty crept in as she watched this man she hadn't seen for years, years that had altered her world irreversibly. Regardless of what he'd gone through in his life, he hadn't experienced the fear of raising a child alone, or the worry that someone might try to take that child away.

Yet, somehow, she couldn't turn from him, from the unexpected opportunity to see for herself what he was like and if he still cared for her.

"I know you're married, but I wanted to see you, to hear how you're doing." He moved toward her, and for one glorious moment, she could believe there was a connection between them that was truly unshakable.

"My life was never the same after you walked away," she said, her words muffled by a strange tightness in her throat.

"You don't know how much I regret what I did," he said, reaching for her hands.

"Me, too," she whispered.

"Olivia, I've missed you so much," he murmured, his hands closing in on hers.

Her name on his lips brought her comfort, but a voice in her head warned her not to let him touch her. "Don't, James, please don't."

His hands stopped their movement. "Are you all right with this? With us meeting this way?"

She shifted on the sofa but couldn't bring herself to get up. "I'm…not sure. I have a life…."

"I know you do." He moved closer yet, his scent arousing a need she'd fought to bury for so long. All the years of yearning came back in a rush of emotion so intense, Olivia could barely breathe.

All the memories of those nights when she'd lain awake in bed at her aunt's house, and lived with the kind of loneliness that had nearly destroyed her.

And now James was here, an arm's length away. Everything she'd ever dreamed of was just inches from her grasp.

She would give her soul to turn back the clock, to regain the freedom to choose her path. But circumstances had taken that from her. "James, we can't do this. Nothing's changed for us, has it?"

He placed his arm along the back of the sofa as he moved closer. "Oh God, Olivia, how did this happen?" he asked, his lips hovering over hers.

"I thought my life was over when you left," she whispered. "I still don't understand why you didn't—"

"Shh." His fingers touched her lips, and she was suddenly dizzy with the intensity of her feelings.

"You can't imagine how many times I wondered where you were, what you were doing, if you were happy," she said, her body moving toward his, her fingers clutching the open collar of his cotton shirt.

His lips were on hers, and his hands slipped around her, pulling her against him. Drowning in her need for him, for his strength, she welcomed his touch. Her fingers trembled as they worked open the buttons of his shirt. His groan of excitement only intensified her need.

"Olivia," he whispered against her throat, his lips trailing over her neck, along her chin to her mouth.

Thoughts of Alex invaded her mind. Alex, the one man who'd willingly stood by her. The man who loved her son as if he were his own flesh and blood. Alex trusted her and relied on her—as she relied on him. She moved away a little. "James, this isn't right. We can't do this without others being hurt, and I'm not prepared to take the chance without knowing—"

"You deserve to be happy."

As she let her gaze linger on his face, she felt his power over her. And if she succumbed to her attraction to James, she'd cause Alex so much pain and heartache. "We have to be completely sure of our feelings for each other. I can't leave that easily. I have my family to protect. My husband…"

He looked at her as if she'd struck him. "I don't want to hurt anyone, either, but some things are out of our control."

"No." She shook her head. "We can't."

"Olivia, I want us to have a future together. Are you willing to waste more of our lives?"

"My life hasn't been a waste," she said angrily, thinking of her son.

He sighed. "I didn't mean that the way it came out. But we have this time together to decide how we want to live the rest of our lives. Let's make the most of it."

"James," she said, unable to ignore the past, "your father's wishes meant more to you than I did."

"No, Olivia, but we were young, and I thought I couldn't defy my father. I made a mistake. A mistake I've been paying for ever since."

"We've both been paying for."

He nodded and the sorrow on his face was almost more than she could bear. But sorrow wouldn't change anything.

"While you were obeying your father's commands, I was living in a different world."

"Olivia, I'd nearly given up hope that you and I would ever be together when I ran into Grace at Dad's funeral. She told me where you were. I needed to see you, to know what was going on in your life. To make sure you're happy. I don't want to hurt you. I've done enough of that."

His eyes radiated pain and loneliness…and love.

"Maybe we do have another chance," Olivia said, her chin tilted up, her gaze direct. She owed Alex her loyalty but she couldn't give him her heart. James had that….

WHY HAD he waited so long? What had made him think life would stop for Olivia just because he'd asked her to wait? "Olivia, I wish you'd come to see me when I sent you the ticket."

She closed her eyes, and when she opened them again, they glistened with tears. "I couldn't leave…. You didn't say you wanted to marry me. I knew that if I went, my marriage would be over. I'd devastate my husband, and he and I could both end up miserable. To leave and go to you, to ruin my life without knowing… The risk—"

"Was too great." He knew all about risk and the fear it created.

"Olivia, I need you to understand that I never meant to hurt you," he said clearly. "I just couldn't see my way out of the situation back then."

"And now with your father gone, you've decided to return to me." Her quiet tone belied the hope he saw in her eyes.

He'd wanted nothing more than to take her in his arms and make love to her—with no complications, no regrets.

That would have happened years ago, when he believed she'd wait for him. "When did you get married?" he asked suddenly.

"October, 1967."

"That same year?" he asked, his voice flat with disbelief.

She nodded, but didn't meet his eyes.

She'd married just four months after he'd left. "And all that time, I thought you were willing to wait for me," he said bleakly.

"I couldn't."

"Or wouldn't," he countered, all hope draining from him. "So, you were already married when I sent you the airline ticket."

She nodded.

"Why didn't you tell me back then?"

"I couldn't."

"Why not?"

She didn't reply.

If Olivia had waited, if she'd been willing to believe and trust in him, in their lives together… "Would you leave your life behind for me now?"

He saw the truth in her eyes.

Tears soaked her eyelashes as Olivia continued to stare at him. "Oh, James, why didn't you call me or try to contact me when you got to Ireland? I called your house and they told me you'd left. I felt completely abandoned by you. I survived that and now you want me to pick up and leave the life I've made for myself."

Seeing the sorrow in her eyes, James faced the fact that he was making a fool of himself by being here. "Olivia, I've never wanted anyone but you, and I never will."

"That was true years ago, James," she said with finality.

But it hadn't changed anything for them. Was that what she was trying to tell him? "You're right. I have no business asking you to leave your life behind for me."

Her cheeks damp with tears, Olivia murmured, "I'd give anything if we could go back, start over."

He breathed in her scent, clinging to the moment, knowing it was over between them. "But we can't, can we?"

FROM THE MOMENT she'd told him when she got married, everything had changed. The anger and betrayal she saw in his eyes was unfair and undeserved, but she wouldn't defend herself to him.

Back then, she'd had no choice but to protect Kyle from the shame of illegitimacy, and she'd protect him again.

Her heart ached to tell James about his son, but telling him was out of the question now.

The trust between them was damaged beyond repair. Telling James about Kyle wouldn't change anything... except Kyle's life.

And Alex's.

As much as she loved James, it was Alex who'd given her a second chance, had saved her from the shame of being an unwed mother. He was Kyle's dad in every way but one. She owed Alex so much, and she cared for him deeply. "We'd hurt so many people," she said, wiping the tears that flowed down her cheeks.

"What about us?

"I shouldn't have come here," she said. But she hadn't been able to resist. In the end, her responsibility to Alex and, above all, Kyle won out.

Kyle had become a headstrong teenager, and Alex was the only person he'd listen to. They needed each other, those two. "What would our life together be like if it was built on the pain of others?"

"What about *our* pain? Our dreams?"

"Maybe that's all it was meant to be—a dream. Maybe you and I missed our chance." She heard his sudden intake of breath and saw the desolation in his eyes.

James rose and stood looking down at her. "I can't do this, Olivia. I can't say goodbye," he said so softly she could hardly hear him.

Unable to bear the regret she saw on his face, she closed her eyes. The creak of the floorboards and the squeal of hinges told her he'd left the cottage.

On the way home, her car radio detailed the events surrounding the shuttle *Challenger* and its horrible fall from the sky. January 28, 1986—a day she'd remember for the rest of her life.

CHAPTER ELEVEN

OVER THE MONTHS that followed, Olivia never quite managed to put James out of her mind. She found herself reading the Boston papers again, looking for news of him.

For a few weeks after they'd met at the cottage, she raced for the phone whenever it rang, hoping somehow that it would be James. When her mother casually mentioned during a phone call that James had gone back to Ireland, Olivia felt empty, drained.

Then, one morning in mid-July, Olivia was loading the dishwasher after getting breakfast for Alex and Kyle....

"Olivia, honey, Kyle and I are going to Fenway Park for the game." Alex came around the breakfast table, to kiss her cheek. "Don't save dinner for us, we're eating out," he said, winking at Kyle who waited impatiently by the door.

"Have a good time," she said.

Through the window, she watched them leave,

smiled at the casual sauntering walk they shared. Kyle had taken on so many of Alex's mannerisms that no one would suspect they weren't related by blood. They told the same jokes, loved the same sports, gobbled down chocolate sundaes and spent Saturday morning playing video games. Their favorite pastime was teasing her about her lack of housekeeping skills. She retaliated by making them hand-dig a flower bed, or move a shrub.

The three of them were a great team. Alex and Kyle made her world a safe haven.

Since her meeting with James in January and her disappointment with how it had ended, Olivia had come to feel a quiet contentment. All the guilt she'd endured over not telling James about Kyle had subsided. Seeing James at the cottage and realizing that their chance for happiness was gone, she'd been able to accept that she and James would never be together.

She turned from the window and retrieved the paper from the hall table. As usual, she started flipping through the pages, scanning the headlines. It wasn't until she got to the society page that she stopped.

A full-length photo of James and Grace, smiling at each other, leaped up at her. She sank into the love seat. A sense of unreality flowed over her as she read the marriage announcement.

They'd been married a week ago in Barbados. The article went on to describe the number of attendees and the bride and groom's plans to take up residence in Ireland.

James had married Grace barely six months after he'd told Olivia he wanted her, and only her. Had he been seeing Grace all this time? How had he changed his feelings so quickly?

"He married Grace," she whispered to the empty room.

She braced herself for the tears that wouldn't come. The announcement destroyed her defenses against the unfailing hope that, despite everything, she and James would find their way back together.

The one man she'd ever truly loved, had married the one woman who knew just how cruel that would be. Granted, she hadn't been willing to run from her own obligations. But now she felt finally and inevitably alone.

The worst feeling in the world.

She wanted to cry, to rail at the fate that had left her out of James's life. Yet she had to face the fact that she'd made her choice a long time ago. She'd decided to marry Alex, rather than even attempt to follow James to Ireland. She'd chosen a world of safety and predictability, and traded love for caring.

With grim determination, she crumpled up the

paper and tossed it in the garbage. She would make the best of everything she had in her life.

From here on, she would be the best wife any man could ask for. She would make sure that Alex was happy with her and with their life together.

"I DIDN'T KNOW how unhappy *I* would be," Olivia murmured as she smoothed the hair off James's forehead.

The nurses had given her permission to sit with him for longer periods, and she'd taken advantage of the opportunity to spend every possible second with her husband.

"What did you say?" James asked, really smiling at her for the first time.

Olivia smiled back at him. "Nothing for you to worry about, darling. You just rest and get better. I see a little more color in your cheeks today, and Dr. Crealock seems to think you're making progress."

"That's good," James said, his eyes locked on hers. "I want to get out of here and go home with you. This is no damned fun." Rolling his eyes, he glanced around the Intensive Care cubicle.

"You'll be home soon, I promise."

"I'd better be," he said with mock ferocity.

"What would I do without you?" she asked, knowing the answer only too well. She'd been miserable for years without him. She'd thought her life with Alex was all she could ever expect.

"*You're* going to get me out of here," James said, raising his hand to hold hers against his cheek.

"Well, then, you'd better rest up, because when you get home, I'm not letting you out of my sight ever again," Olivia said, remembering a different day when she'd lived with enough lost hope to last her a lifetime.

OLIVIA WAS looking forward to using her college skills at the restaurant now that her degree was finally finished. She'd completed all her courses on a part-time basis over the past decade or so, a course or two a year. So it was with complete disillusionment that she found herself embroiled, yet again, in another argument with her husband.

"Olivia, why do you want to work full-time in the restaurant? We've got all the money we'll ever need. We deserve to live a little," Alex said.

It was spiteful of her to think this way, but she wouldn't be having this argument if she'd been married to James. He'd told her over and over how smart she was, how proud he was of her. He'd believed in her, telling her constantly that someday she'd change the world. She'd never quite believed *that,* but it was his faith in her that counted.

"Alex, *you're* still involved in your businesses. What if I objected to you working?"

Alex ran his hands through his gray hair. "It's not the same, Olivia. Why don't you relax and enjoy life?"

After initially agreeing to her plans to attend college part-time, Alex had resisted her efforts to pursue a career, especially one that involved Crawford's Steak House.

Olivia had just celebrated her fortieth birthday, and with the realization that there'd be no children, their relationship had become one of polite and pleasant distance.

She supposed that a lot of married couples eventually took each other for granted, but in her mind, their gradual withdrawal had been going on for a very long time.

Their life together always seemed much easier as friends and coworkers than as lovers. Being lovers had always been fraught with the tension of whether or not she'd get pregnant. Alex had made no secret of his disappointment over not having children.

"Alex, I love the restaurant business. I have ever since I first worked at Crawford's."

"Yes, and it shows. Even with you working only a couple of days a week, we've never done better," he grudgingly admitted.

"Then maybe we should consider expanding, perhaps franchising. There are so many great opportunities out there." She slid onto the sofa beside him, reaching for his hand.

"Olivia, I don't want to talk about this." Instead of taking her hand as he usually did, he moved away.

She experienced a feeling of shock at his behavior. It wasn't like Alex to be quite this remote.

"I don't want to argue, either, but you're not being fair."

He gave her an exasperated glance as he rose from the sofa. "Fine," he snapped. "If that's what you want, I'll make arrangements for you to start full-time at the beginning of next month. It means I'll have to put Miranda back to evening shift manager, but that's the way it is."

Feeling guilty, she watched him leave the house without turning back for his usual goodbye kiss. Alex's idea of a job for Olivia was to become a volunteer and take over his mother's position in the community, left vacant when she entered the nursing home.

But volunteering bored Olivia. It held none of the excitement of the day-to-day problem-solving involved in running a restaurant. She'd rather donate her earnings to a worthy cause and spend her time pursuing a challenging job.

Besides, with Kyle in university, staying home was lonely. She should be glad, she guessed, that Kyle had decided on a career. He wanted to be an anthropologist, and he'd focused all his studies in that area.

The doorbell interrupted her thoughts. "I'm coming," she called, thinking Alex must have forgotten something.

She strode down the hall and opened the door. "Grace!" she gasped in surprise.

"May I come in?" Grace asked, shifting her weight from one elegantly shod foot to the other.

Olivia smothered the old feelings of betrayal and forced a smile. Needless to say, the last person she'd expected to see was Grace Underhill. No, Grace McElroy. "H-how did you find me?" she stammered.

"I asked your mother."

She wanted to ask where James was, but didn't. James was no longer her business. "What are you doing here?"

"May I come in?" Grace asked again, looking past her toward the interior of the house.

As she stared at her friend, she had to admit to being a *little* curious. "Of course." Olivia moved aside and let her pass.

Grace made for the sofa so recently vacated by Alex, and slid into its depths, her rail-thin body making only the slightest indentation in the cushions.

"Are you alone, Olivia?"

"Alex is at work. Why do you ask?"

"I've missed you. I came to make peace with you, to apologize and see if we can be friends again."

"Why now?" Olivia asked.

"I wish we'd stayed in touch. When you disappeared after high school, my life wasn't much fun without you. I didn't like college. I tried out for the volleyball team but didn't make the cut. I spent most of my college years in one destructive relationship after another. Unfortunately, my years of expensive therapy didn't change my attitude toward men. Olivia, no one knows better than I do what a mess I can make of my life…without even trying. I've never had a friend like you. I've missed you so much."

Grace's face held hope and remorse in equal measure, and Olivia was powerless to resist her plea. After all the years of being apart, and all the times Olivia had wanted to call Grace, Olivia was filled with a strange sense of coming home….

"I've missed you, too, Grace," she said fervently. "You can't imagine how often I thought of calling you."

Sitting down on the edge of the sofa, she wrapped her arms around Grace.

"Oh, Olivia, how did we end up like this?" Grace asked, hugging her so tightly Olivia could feel her bones.

Grace's sudden burst of sobbing echoed through Olivia. "What's wrong?"

Grace looked up. "You know James and I got married?"

Olivia nodded.

"He left me. We were getting ready to celebrate our fourth wedding anniversary when he came home and told me he wanted a divorce," Grace said, her voice shaking. "He doesn't love me anymore, but I can't live without him. I can't go on if he doesn't love me. I *can't*."

Pity—and fear for Grace—touched Olivia as she gazed into her friend's teary eyes. "Grace, it can't be that bad. You and James love each other. You have so much in common."

"Tell *him* that." Grace pulled a tissue from her bag and wiped her eyes.

Olivia felt confused by her contradictory reactions, but her first priority was to comfort Grace. "Come on. I'll make us a pot of tea. You still like tea, don't you?" Olivia asked, leading her to the brightness of the kitchen.

Going through the familiar motions of making tea had a soothing effect on both of them. Wanting to dispel the anxiety in Grace's eyes, Olivia took the tea tray out to the patio. "I always feel better out here. It's the fresh air, the sunshine…."

"And all the birds you attract to your bird feeders. I see you haven't lost your love of birds." Grace glanced at the garden as she sat down. "Or the vegetable garden."

"Yeah, Dad got me started on vegetable gardening."

"I went to see your mom and dad. They've been so good to me. They told me where you lived. I hope that's okay," she added tentatively.

"Of course. I should've been in touch with you myself, years ago."

Over tea, they talked about their lives, about how much they'd missed each other. "I wish we'd stayed in contact," Olivia said. "It's my fault we didn't. I was just so ashamed…."

"You? Ashamed? What would *you* have to be ashamed of?" Grace held her teacup in both hands as she frowned across the patio table at Olivia.

Olivia was tempted to confide in her friend, to tell her the truth about Kyle. "So, do you and James still talk?" she asked instead.

"No. He doesn't take my calls anymore." Grace put her cup down. "I tried to stop the divorce, but he wouldn't hear of it. I wanted us to stay married, to try to reconcile. I would've done anything—" Tears choked off her words. "He said there wasn't anyone else, but I don't believe him. I'll never accept that he didn't leave me for another woman. He couldn't just leave me…."

"Grace, I wish I knew how to help you," Olivia said, taking her friend's hands in hers.

"You'd tell me if James had talked to you about our marriage, wouldn't you? And if you knew who he was seeing, you'd tell me, right?"

"Why would you think I'd even seen him? What gave you that idea?"

"Well…you were always so close…."

Was that why Grace was here, to find out if James was in touch with her? Or maybe Grace thought *she* was the other woman?

No, Grace is your friend, and she's in trouble. "Of course, I'd tell you if I knew anything. But I don't. James and I haven't spoken in years."

CHAPTER TWELVE

"THANK YOU for that." Grace smoothed her hair away from her face. "I need to tell you something, something I'm not very proud of."

"What?"

"James told me about how his father made him leave and go to Ireland. He wouldn't tell me what happened, other than to say that his father found out about you and him. I didn't know your relationship was a secret, I swear I didn't."

Olivia gave Grace a wry smile. "I didn't, either."

"You're kidding."

Olivia shook her head, remembering that June night with sadness.

"Anyway, the Christmas before your breakup, I went to the company Christmas party, and I blabbed to James's father. I was so nervous back then, and so anxious to make a good impression on Mr. McElroy. After all, he was my father's boss. And of course there was the whole thing about James and me."

"What thing?" Olivia asked.

"You know that Mom and Dad assumed James and I would get married someday and live happily ever after." Grace frowned. "So much for that idea."

"No, I didn't know."

"Anyway, that Christmas I talked to James's father about how you and James were dating, and how exciting it was, how much in love you were. For the first time since I'd met Tom McElroy, he gave me his complete attention. I was young, impressionable and so flattered. I told him everything I knew."

"Grace, you didn't!"

"I did, and I blame myself for what went wrong between the two of you, because when James told me…I realized that his father had no intention of letting James see you after graduation. But I never meant to hurt you or James. I thought it was harmless gossip. James was furious when I told him what I'd done."

Disappointment and disbelief tore at Olivia. Had James let her believe the worst when he could have eased her pain with only a few words of explanation?

"Grace," she began after a long silence, "please don't feel responsible for what happened. James and I saw each other a few years ago, before you were married, and we both decided it wouldn't have worked."

"You did? He didn't tell me that. Why would he keep it a secret from me? I was his wife, and you and I were friends. I don't get it."

"We talked, that's all."

"Why didn't you get back together? What stopped you?"

"Our lives had changed, I guess, and I was married with a son."

"A son? Your mother didn't mention a child. Did James know about your son?"

She wanted so much to confide in someone about Kyle and who his father was. "No, I didn't tell him about Kyle."

"Why not? He would've understood."

"I couldn't. I didn't want James asking questions I couldn't answer, not without hurting people."

"Alex isn't Kyle's father?" The look of surprise on Grace's face turned to realization. "Kyle is James's son."

Anxiety spiked through Olivia, followed quickly by a sense of relief. "Yes, he is."

Grace's expression was one of sympathy as she came around the table and hugged Olivia. "It must've been hard for you to see James and not tell him. How did you manage it?"

"I don't know. I hadn't seen James in so long, and when I finally did…"

"What'd he say?"

"He was kind, but very disappointed that I hadn't waited for him. I couldn't tell him why I got married so soon after he left. I couldn't tell him about Kyle without knowing how he really felt about me. So much had changed. Eventually I had to accept that what we had together had been lost."

"It must have been so difficult to walk away."

Olivia nodded, her heart thudding painfully at the memory. "I should've told James from the beginning, but when he went to Ireland and didn't come back for me…I had to protect Kyle. I had to make a life for my son."

"And you did." Grace glanced around at the beautifully tended gardens and the elegant brick exterior of the house. "You made a wonderful life for him."

"And Alex has been so kind, so good to Kyle. Kyle loves him." Olivia swallowed hard, willing herself not to succumb to her feelings of regret.

HOURS LATER, after Grace had gone, Alex and Olivia sat on the deck enjoying the sunset. They'd been talking about Grace's sudden appearance.

"You were so quiet during dinner, and you didn't have much to say to Grace, Alex. She was my best friend in high school, and I'm so glad she's come to visit. Once you get to know her, you'll really like her."

Alex grimaced and sent Olivia a piercing look she'd hadn't seen before. "Why did you tell Grace about Kyle's father?"

"How did you know?"

"I came home and overheard you and Grace on the patio." He swallowed hard. "I know James McElroy still matters to you from the way you talked about him."

"You were eavesdropping!"

"Hardly. You were so involved in the conversation you didn't even hear me come in. Admit it. You want him back in your life."

"No, I don't—"

"Olivia, please, after all we've meant to each other, don't pretend with me. You were honest about Kyle's father before we got married. What I want to know is why Grace was here, and why you were so quick to confide in her about your past life. That was our secret. And what about Kyle? What if he finds out?"

"He won't."

"How do you know that? Your friend is angry about her divorce and looking for a way to get back at her husband. How can you be sure she won't use what she knows? Telling a childless man—the same man who divorced her—that he has a son would be quite a coup for Grace."

Why had she been so stupid? Grace had told James's father about their relationship; what guarantee did Olivia have that she wouldn't tell James about Kyle? "Alex, Grace wouldn't do that," she said uncertainly. "I'll talk to her."

"And what about me? Where does that leave me?"

Olivia cringed. She'd been too wrapped up in having someone to confide in. "I couldn't hurt you like that. I care too much about you…about us."

"But don't you see? You *are* hurting me by bringing a woman into this house who is part of your past with James. You want Grace around because she's your connection to James."

"That's not true! How can you say that?"

"Because I see it in your eyes, the way you behave with Grace. She's your link to the past."

"Alex, Grace was married to James. They just got divorced. End of story."

"I doubt that's the end of the story, not by a long shot," Alex said, his gaze hard. "Maybe *you* want a divorce."

"No! I don't want a divorce."

"Then what *do* you want?"

Why was he saying these things? Had he been as unsure as she had all these years? "Alex, I want the life we have together," she said, and at that moment she meant it. "I want Grace to be part of it. I've missed her. We always had such fun together, and I miss that. In all the years since we've been apart, I've never found a friend like her. She's not going to tell James about Kyle and she's not going to change anything between you and me."

"Things have already changed between us, Olivia. I love you, but I can't go on, thinking that you're still in love with James McElroy. If you can tell me with complete honesty that you have no feelings for him, then I'm willing to work at our marriage."

"Work at our marriage?"

"Yes. I wanted children of our own. I'd hoped for a big family. I figured the reason we didn't have kids was that you didn't want to have them with me."

"You're not being fair!"

"Then why did I so often see anxiety rather than pleasure in your eyes when we made love?"

"That's not true."

Liar, liar, whispered a voice deep inside her. As much as she denied his words, some part of her had secretly acknowledged how empty she felt when she and Alex made love.

"I want you to be happy, Alex, and I want to be your wife."

"But you still can't say you love me. After all this time, you can't speak the words."

The truth of what he said hung silent between them.

"I could accept that you didn't love me as long as you could put me first in your life."

"I do put you first, you know that!" Olivia replied, exasperated with Alex's attack on her motives, despite her own doubts.

"Then, don't invite Grace here again."

"I didn't!"

"I don't mind you seeing her when you go to Boston, or for the occasional weekend, but she cannot be in our lives here in Bar Harbor. She's part of James's life, and I won't have you anywhere near the man who abandoned you when you needed him most."

Alex rose and stood over her. "Think about it, Olivia. If I hadn't been there for you, what would've become of you and Kyle?"

FOR WEEKS afterward, Olivia struggled with the confused feelings she'd experienced after she and Alex had their argument over Grace. She'd given in to Alex's demand that Grace not be invited to their home, but in the act of denying her friend, she'd seen what her life had become.

She had lived a life of denial. First she'd denied

being left to raise a child alone by stubbornly believing that James would be back. Then she'd denied the heartache of a marriage that wasn't based on love.

Although Alex's insistence that Grace not return had started all this soul-searching, there was a new yearning for James that haunted every moment of her life.

Alex was right. Everything about her relationship with Grace reminded her of James and the love they'd once shared.

She'd hidden away their love, denied it. And that was the biggest denial of all.

Hopeless and futile as the situation was, she could no longer ignore her feelings for James. She might spend the rest of her life wanting him, and she probably would. But there was no reason Alex should suffer because of her mistake.

And marrying Alex when she didn't love him had been a mistake.

Her willingness to avoid the truth had cost her husband his happiness. More than anything in this world, she wanted Alex to be happy. With everything he'd done for her, and all the love and care he'd lavished on Kyle, Alex deserved to be with someone who truly loved him.

BUT ALEX and Olivia continued to share a life together over the next two months. Alex was considerate to a fault, but nothing more. And when he came home late from a business meeting, he'd often go to bed in the guest suite. Yet neither one took any action to change the situation.

Life would probably have continued that way if it hadn't been for an urgent call from Grace. She'd broken her ankle and asked Olivia to visit her in New York.

Olivia and Alex had settled in to read after dinner when she brought up the subject. "I want to go to New York to see Grace. And I'll visit Mom and Dad in Frampton on the way home," she said, glancing across the living room at her husband.

"I think you should. It will give us both time away from each other, to decide what we want."

His words shocked her. Although she'd come to accept that some sort of separation was inevitable, what had held her back had been her fear of hurting Alex. "Are you sure?"

"Olivia, what I said when Grace was here still stands. You and I have had a good life together."

"Yes, we have."

"But things don't always turn out the way we want, and we need to face reality—as much as we care for each other, as much as we want our son to have the happiness he deserves, we can't continue like this."

Olivia stared unseeing at the book in her lap. Alex was saying the words she couldn't say.

"Look at me, Olivia," he urged, crossing the living room and sitting down beside her. "I want us to remain friends, to be Kyle's parents. But if we go on like this, we'll hurt each other in ways we can't even imagine. When you married me you were completely honest about your feelings, and now I need to be completely honest with you."

Olivia swallowed over the lump wedged in her throat. "You've always been honest with me."

Alex shook his head as he took her hand in his. "Not always. Marrying you and being Kyle's father allowed me to make peace with what I'd done to Anna and my son. Aside from that, I'll admit I wanted a certain social standing, which included a wife who was content to stay at home. At times, I resented your abilities, and that wasn't fair."

Mutely she shook her head.

"Olivia, you've been so kind to me, so supportive. Now I want you to follow your dream—whatever that means for you."

"Alex, I wish things were different. I wish I could love you the way you deserve to be loved."

"What we have is good." His smile was sad. "But it isn't enough for either of us."

If only she could tell Alex how deeply she appreciated him. But her tears were too close. "What will you do?"

"Pretty much the same as I'm doing now. I'm going to focus on the car dealerships and try to find balance in my life."

"And Kyle?"

"He's due home this weekend. We'll talk to him then."

Sadness settled around Olivia's heart. The life they'd shared was over. "Alex, you know how hard my life would've been if you hadn't come to my rescue. You saved me and our son from a very difficult situation, and I will never forget that."

The hand holding hers trembled as he kissed her forehead. "I know, Olivia. I know…"

They talked to Kyle that weekend and he said he was okay with it. But both Alex and Olivia learned otherwise when the police escorted an inebriated Kyle home in the early hours of Sunday morning. And for a while, both Alex and Olivia feared that Kyle might be headed for serious trouble.

Kyle blamed his mother for the divorce. His words of anger and condemnation accompanied her every move during the weeks and months following the decision to separate.

But again, Alex had come to her rescue and talked to Kyle. Olivia was relieved that she and Alex were able to discuss him. Strange as it seemed, once they separated they were better friends than when they'd been married.

Being open and honest about her feelings where Alex was concerned had freed Olivia to enjoy the daily routine of the restaurant business while the separation and divorce played themselves out.

Today, she stared down at the documents in front of her, a pen between her fingers. All she had to do was sign the paperwork and allow Alex his freedom. Alex and her…

It seemed so simple, so easy. Yet it had taken a year to work out the details of their separate lives. A year during which Olivia faced her parents and her friends in Bar Harbor, none of whom understood why she and Alex were getting a divorce. Everyone thought their marriage was solid, and in so many ways it had been.

Despite her newfound sense of confidence, fear of the unknown assailed her as she scribbled her signature on the divorce documents and passed them back to her lawyer.

SEEKING THE HEAT of the late-March sun, Olivia lingered on the steps of the old stone building that housed her lawyer's office.

She couldn't go home just yet. Although Alex had taken his personal belongings, there were still so many memories behind the walls of the home she and Alex had shared.

They'd agreed that Olivia would get the house and the restaurant, while Alex kept the car dealerships. Her lawyer had pushed her to fight for a greater percentage of Alex's assets, but Olivia couldn't do that. Alex had already given her more than money could ever buy. The other financial arrangements allowed Kyle to continue at Western Michigan University.

She decided to leave her car in the parking lot and walk down to the restaurant. In anticipation of the night ahead, Olivia hurried along the narrow street, the smell of the sea filling her nostrils.

She'd grown to love Bar Harbor, its quaint shops and postage-stamp parks. She'd been working at the restaurant full-time for nearly five years, and tonight the bustle of the dinner hour was a balm to the anxiety she'd struggled with all day.

Although it was still early for dinner, everywhere she looked there were tables of people laughing and enjoying each other's company. She envied them.

"Hi, Olivia." Max Sutherland and his elderly mother waved from their usual booth near the door as she went by.

She waved back, making her way through the dining room to her office at the rear. It was shaping up to be a busy night, and she planned to be part of it.

"You've had a phone call from someone at Laurel Industries," Miranda said, balancing a loaded tray on her shoulders as she swept past Olivia. "I left the number on your desk. The guy said he'd be at the office till at least seven."

Olivia had put all her business acumen to work, looking for someone to help finance her plans to franchise the restaurant. Laurel Industries, an international conglomerate, had been one of the companies recommended by her banker as a potential investor. Although she wasn't familiar with Laurel, she'd sent her proposal to them several months ago, but hadn't heard back. "Thanks, Miranda."

Once she was settled at her desk, Olivia grabbed the piece of paper with the number on it and dialed.

"Laurel Industries," a man with a deep voice answered.

"I'm sorry to bother you this late in the day, but I'd like to speak to a Mr. Hammond."

"You got him. I'm Jake Hammond."

"I'm Olivia Crawford. I own Crawford's Restaurant in Bar Harbor."

"Thanks for getting back to me. Your request for financing was brought to my attention, and we'd like a chance to talk to you, to get a better idea of what you're looking for."

Much to her chagrin, all the local investors had turned down her proposal. The business community here tended to be conservative, and she suspected that a female entrepreneur held little appeal for those who wanted a sure thing in the world of investing. On top of that, many of the potential investors were loyal to Alex, which prevented them from getting involved. "I really appreciate your interest in what I'm proposing," she said excitedly.

She explained the basics of what she hoped to do and answered his questions. "Is there any other information you need?"

"Could you meet with us sometime tomorrow?"

"That soon?" What was she saying? She could meet anytime.

"The sooner the better, I'd say."

"Just tell me where and when," she said, opening her day timer.

CHAPTER THIRTEEN

THE NEXT MORNING at ten o'clock, she stood at the entrance to an office suite in downtown Boston. She'd stayed up most of the night, going over her plans, refining her pitch to Mr. Hammond. It felt so good to be given the opportunity to do this.

Taking a deep breath, she opened the door and approached the receptionist, a beautiful brunette with dark eyes and a bright smile.

"I'm Olivia Crawford," she said, "and I'm here to see Mr. Hammond."

"Certainly. I'll let them know you're here. Please have a seat," the young woman told her, picking up the phone.

"MRS. CRAWFORD'S here," Jake Hammond said, putting down the phone.

James glanced up from the documents he'd been trying to show some interest in for the past half hour. He'd been relieved and yet anxious when he learned that Olivia had agreed to come to the meeting today.

He'd berated himself for letting her leave the cottage without him that day six years before. And then the mistake he'd made in marrying Grace... He groaned inwardly.

He'd made so many mistakes where Olivia was concerned, and now he worried that if today didn't go well, he would've made the biggest mistake of all.

"I'm to disappear the minute she comes through the door, correct?" Positioning himself by the door, Jake smiled and checked his watch. "Which should be right about now."

As if on cue, the door opened, and Olivia strode into the dimly lit room. "Mr. Hammond? Thank you for seeing me," she said, extending her hand.

"It's our pleasure," Jake said. "I'd like to introduce the CEO of Laurel Industries."

A small gasp escaped Olivia's lips as she met James's eyes. "I didn't know..."

He stood up, nearly knocking over his chair. "Hello, Olivia, it's good to see you again," he said, feeling awkward as fear ran unfettered through him. Fear that she'd turn and walk out. Fear that he'd face the rest of his life without her. And never know his son.

"James, what are *you* doing here?" Olivia asked, her face flushed, her eyes bright.

His hands ached to touch her. Blood pounded

in his head, and the doctor's warning rang in his ears. "I own the company," he said, offering her the chair next to his.

Hesitantly, Olivia moved toward him. "My...my bank recommended you. I didn't check— I should've known," she said when she reached him.

The light floral scent he remembered so well suffused the air around them, while James let the idea sink in that she was actually here. "I hope you don't mind, but I wanted to talk to you—person-ally—about your plans."

"Is that all?" she asked, her gaze piercing his defenses.

"No, that's not all. I need to talk to you about something else, something important.... Please sit down." He held out the chair for her.

"Olivia, I hardly know where to start. There's so much I need to tell you, so much I need to apologize for," he said.

"Go on." He saw a look of bewilderment in her eyes.

"Olivia, Grace went to visit you, didn't she?"

Olivia's face paled. "When did you see her?"

"She was visiting my mother. She told me Kyle's my son." *There, it was out in the open.*

Her eyes widened in surprise. "I wanted to tell you a long time ago."

"Why didn't you?"

Despite the anxiety in her eyes, her voice didn't waver. "Because I couldn't bring myself to hurt my family."

"I see." He didn't see at all, but he needed to hear about his son. "You were protecting them."

"Please understand. I was alone and pregnant, with no one to turn to except my parents, who wanted me to put Kyle up for adoption. I did what I believed was best for my son." She frowned, creating a tiny furrow between her eyes.

James wished he could touch the frown, ease the tension he saw there, but he was powerless to move. He remembered the joy he'd experienced when Grace had told him about Kyle. A joy that quickly turned to sorrow at what had been lost.

"For *our* son, you mean," he said.

"Yes, for our son. I felt responsible…."

"But so was I. You didn't make that baby by yourself." He tried for a smile and was relieved to see her lips curve up at the corners.

"But I had so many things to worry about once I learned I was pregnant, and moving to Bar Harbor was frightening. I didn't know a soul there, only my aunt and uncle, who weren't very happy to see me."

"And you never tried to contact me, let me share in the responsibility for Kyle?" he asked.

"How could I with your father's threat to ruin my parents hanging over me?"

James muttered something she didn't hear.

"Your family wouldn't tell me how to get in touch with you. My parents were mortified that their only daughter was expecting a child out of wedlock and the father had abandoned her. They did what they could to find me a place to have the baby. If my aunt and uncle hadn't been willing to help out, I don't know where I would've ended up. When Kyle was almost four, I called your house, but your mother refused to tell me anything."

A pain shot through his chest, and he clenched his jaw to ward it off. "If only I'd known. I should've been there for you. Instead, you had to raise our child alone." He could think of little that would defend what his family had done to him, to her, and now to his son.

Olivia gripped the edge of the teak table, her eyes dark with memories. "You don't know how often I wanted to call again, but I didn't dare."

"When you told me you'd married only four months after I left, I was angry that you hadn't waited for me." He shook his head. "I should've trusted you. I should've known there was a very powerful reason you'd decided to marry. But it never occurred to me. How could I have been so damned stupid?" he asked, easing her fingers away from the edge of the table and covering them with his. He rubbed the warmth back into her cold hands, happy to do something for Olivia at last, however small.

"Oh, James, you'll never know the hours I spent waiting to hear from you. When you sent the airline ticket, I was so excited at the prospect of seeing you. But I couldn't put my happiness ahead of Kyle's. None of this was his fault. And I couldn't betray Alex…."

"I envy him."

Olivia gazed at him, a sad smile on her face. "Alex was very kind to me. I couldn't have made it without him."

She squeezed his hand, and he was suddenly aware that she wasn't wearing a wedding ring. "Is everything all right between you and Alex?"

"We're divorced."

"I'm sorry."

"Are you really?" she asked, her tone skeptical.

"No, I'm sorry you had to go through such a difficult time. But I'm glad you're free."

Hell, he was thrilled. He hadn't been this happy since the afternoon they'd decorated the high school gym. That long-ago day… "I want a second chance," he said abruptly.

"What do you mean?" she asked carefully.

"I want to make up for my mistakes, and give what we had together another chance."

Her eyes brimming with tears, Olivia pulled

her hands from his. "Then why did you let me believe you didn't love me anymore? Why didn't you come home?" Her voice shook.

Overwhelmed by her agony, cursing his stupidity, James took her in his arms.

"I never meant to hurt you, Olivia. Please let me make it up to you."

HIS ARMS were strong, his scent and the beating of his heart filled her with longing for everything they'd been denied, for every lost moment they could have shared. "We can't change the past," she murmured into his chest.

He touched her cheek and tucked a strand of hair behind her ear. "But we can learn from it."

Olivia glanced up into his face. "James, I need time to figure out how I feel about us now."

"How you feel?"

"Yes. I'm just not sure. Our lives are so different—we're different—from what we were twenty-five years ago."

"But if we take our time, get to know each other again… What we had means everything to me."

"You don't understand," she said emphatically, meeting his all-consuming gaze. Finding out about James would only add fuel to Kyle's accusation that she'd been the one to blame for the divorce. "Kyle's been distant with me since the divorce, and now if he finds out about you—"

"Olivia, what can I say that will make a difference?"

"I need you to understand what it's been like for me."

"I'm listening." His broad shoulders offered her protection; the empathy in his eyes urged her on.

"I know I shouldn't be so worried about Kyle. He's a grown man with a life of his own."

"But you do feel responsible."

"I'm the one who kept him from knowing you. I tried to make up for not telling him, and maybe I overcompensated. Not only that, he loves Alex and he's going to feel doubly betrayed."

"Sooner or later, you're going to have to tell him the truth about us," James said, his tone gentle. "Right now may not be ideal, and I respect that, but he *will* have to be told."

Although she accepted what James said, the reality was more difficult. "What will he think of me when we tell him you're his father?"

"He's probably going to be angry that we kept it from him."

"Or worse…"

"I can't believe that a son of yours would refuse to understand. And it's not as if we'd try to push Alex out of his life."

"You don't know Kyle like I do. I love him dearly, but he's very strong-willed."

"Olivia, please trust me." His fingers massaged her shoulders and a once-familiar ache rose through her body. She turned her face to his, tilting her chin to meet his gaze.

"James, this is so hard. You come into my life wanting me to trust you even though I don't know if you'll leave and hurt me again."

"That won't happen. I wanted to see you the minute Grace told me about our son, but I knew that wouldn't be fair. However, I'm going to be part of your life and Kyle's from now on. Make no mistake about that."

"Are you willing to do it my way?"

"Whatever it takes. We could start with me offering you any financial help you need to go ahead with your restaurant plans."

Did he really want to be her business partner? Could she endure letting him into her life when she was afraid he'd just leave her again? Her old insecurities unfurled deep inside her, making her chest feel tight. "Would we be having this conversation if you didn't know about Kyle?" she asked bluntly.

His jaw tensed. "We would've had this conversation years ago if I'd had the courage. If we'd both had…"

He was so close, and yet a chasm of time lay between them. "I'm just beginning to get my life on track again. The timing couldn't be more difficult."

"Olivia, I want to work things out with you."

He'd let his father put her out of his life. He'd married her friend and then divorced her. And now, he expected her to trust him.

How could she?

Yet, she found herself reaching out to him. For years her thoughts had revolved around him, and her marriage had ended because she could no longer deny his role in her life.

Still, her hope of a future with him remained clouded by a memory she couldn't erase—the memory of the night he'd left her without looking back. "I can't accept your offer until I'm sure of who I am and what I want."

His face etched in sorrow, he murmured, "I'll be here whenever you're ready."

Before she could succumb to his charm and persuasiveness and let her life slide out of control, she got up and headed for the door.

CHAPTER FOURTEEN

OLIVIA CLOSED the door of the Intensive Care unit, remembering the day James had come back into her life for good. She searched for Julia among the people in the waiting room, needing someone to offer comfort. James had fallen into a fitful sleep, leaving her alone with her anxious thoughts.

Julia had arrived from New York the day before, and had stayed in James's room last night. With Grace behaving so irrationally, Julia's calm approach was just what Olivia needed.

She and Julia had become friends over the past few years. And she and James had been delighted to be in Julia's wedding party when she married John Talbot a year ago.

"Oh, there you are. How's James?" Grace asked, startling Olivia.

When had Grace come back? "I'm not sure. His breathing's so labored at times, and he seems… agitated, I guess. He's been a little confused, talking about his father."

"What did the doctor say?" Grace asked.

"That he's stable."

"That's it? That's all the doctor told you?"

"Yes."

"I'm going to have this man paged and make him tell us what's going on," she said aggressively.

Olivia frowned at her. "No, you're not. You're going to behave yourself. The doctor's doing his job."

"I want—" Grace's expression went from angry to crestfallen. "There I go again. Your mother warned me not to act like this. I'm making a fool of myself, aren't I? I need to get a grip," she said, looking straight at Olivia.

"Yes, you do. You seem to forget that this is difficult for all of us, Grace."

"Yeah, but especially on you," Grace said gently. "And I'm making it worse."

"We're all trying to cope. Me most of all." Olivia smiled at her friend.

Grace bowed her head. "I have no business being here. You and I are friends, and I want it to stay that way. We've been through too much for me to lose you again."

"Grace, you will never lose me. You might drive me crazy, but you won't lose me."

Grace hugged her. "I'm going home now. Why don't you call me when James is out of the hospital and your life is back to normal. Maybe I'll come and visit you."

"That would be great. We'll be in touch, I promise." Olivia watched Grace leave with a mixture of relief and concern.

"What did *she* want?" Julia asked, coming up beside Olivia, her glance following Grace as she left the waiting room.

"She's worried about James."

"She's worried about Grace, if you ask me."

"Be kind, Julia. Grace is having a hard time."

Julia shrugged, searching the bottom of her huge Gucci bag looking for change. "I'm going to try another of those horrible cups of what passes for coffee from the vending machine. Want one?"

"No, but I'll walk to the machine with you. I'll buy a bottled water."

"I think you should get out of here for a while, take a walk in the park across the street. Maybe even go home for a few hours."

Olivia sighed. "I'd love to, but I keep hoping Kyle will show up. I've left four messages for him, the last one saying I'd like him to come straight to the hospital."

"What do you suppose he's doing over there that would keep him from returning your call?"

"He works long hours for the ski-lift company. I hope it's simply that he's out of cell phone range…."

"I can't imagine how it feels to be looking for your son, and waiting for your husband to recover, all at the same time."

Carrying their drinks, she and Julia walked back along the corridor to the waiting room.

"I'll be so glad when I never have to enter this room again," Olivia said, sitting down near the window.

"I hear you." Julia sank into the seat next to her, a worried expression on her face. "Tell me the truth. Is James going to be all right?"

"I hope so, but the doctors seem unwilling to tell me very much."

"That's so annoying. Why don't they just come out and say what they're thinking?"

"I suppose they don't want to upset the family any more than necessary." In her anxiety, Olivia rubbed her hands, her fingers tracing the emerald-cut diamond and gold band, reminding her how precarious, how unpredictable, life could be.

Only twelve years before, her life had been so different….

OLIVIA CLOSED the file in front of her with a sigh, glancing around her home office as she did so. There'd been no other backers willing to support her plans to franchise, and she was about ready to give up on the idea.

With Kyle away in Michigan, Olivia had little interest in looking after the house, especially the cleaning. The profits from the restaurant made it possible to hire a full-time housekeeper, which was the one luxury Olivia allowed herself.

As for a social life, other than the occasional movie date with a couple of girlfriends, she had none.

The finalization of the divorce had left her a social outcast in Bar Harbor. Their friends now invited Alex to dinner parties where a parade of eligible women vied to become the next Mrs. Crawford.

Several of her friends dropped hints about the latest woman in Alex's life. No one seemed to believe Olivia when she said she hoped he'd find the right woman.

Olivia and Alex talked regularly, especially about Kyle, who was working on his doctorate in anthropology. Meanwhile, her life was one continual round of work and more work. She loved it, but wished she could carry out her plans for the restaurant. The grandfather clock in the hall chimed seven o'clock, reminding her that she'd had nothing to eat since lunch.

She was rummaging in the fridge when the doorbell rang. "Coming," she called. She was expecting an express parcel containing a sportjacket she'd ordered for her father.

She peered through the sidelights, checking for the deliveryman. Standing outside her door, wearing black leather and carrying a helmet under his arm, stood James. In her driveway, the biggest motorcycle she'd ever seen leaned on its kickstand.

Pleasure tempered by anxiety made her hesitate before opening the door. The fact that James was here, on her doorstep, meant only one thing. She opened the door, doing her best to hide her unease.

"It's been a long time since the day I saw you in my office. You didn't get back to me about Kyle, and now you're not returning my business calls, either. So, I decided to do an all-out assault on your home."

He smiled and Olivia's heart gave a funny kick. "I've been busy," she muttered.

He rested one hand high on the door frame and stared down at her. "That covers the business calls, but what about our discussion concerning Kyle? I'm not going to wait much longer."

He was right. She'd been putting it off.

Seeing him standing there sent heat surging through her to the tip of her toes. His shoulders seemed backlit by the low sun reflected off the street. That, and his dark, intent eyes made her one hundred percent aware of just what a gorgeous man he was—and how easily she could slip back into the old feelings of love and need. Feelings that had never really left…

"I haven't eaten yet, and the housekeeper made a beef stew today," she offered.

"You're going to feed me before you send me packing, is that it?" A tentative smile lifted the corners of his mouth.

"We'll see. It depends on what you have to say." She stepped aside to let him into the hall.

"Then I'd better make it good," he said, walking past her, trailing the scent of leather and his cologne.

Acutely aware that James was watching every move, she set the table in the kitchen. All the while, she struggled with what she'd say when he brought up the subject of Kyle.

"If I'd known you'd serve me dinner, I would've brought some wine."

"Not to worry," she said, reaching into the wine rack tucked under the cooking island. "Is a Merlot okay with you?"

"Great." He smiled at her in a way that made her want to snuggle up in his arms. Instead, she took the plates of stew to the table. They ate in silence, the moment becoming more precious to her the longer they sat across from one another.

How many times had she dreamed of this? How many times had she fantasized about what it would be like to sit across from him, enjoying a meal and a glass of wine? Sharing simple pleasures and ordinary days.

"Tell me about your business plan," he said, moving his empty plate aside.

"I put my franchising plans on hold. I still don't have an investor."

"You always have me."

"I haven't made up my mind about you."

He tilted his chin and gave her a grin that made her toes curl. "Well, my offer hasn't changed, and I'm prepared to wait you out," he said, pulling his chair around the table next to hers.

His closeness reminded her of all the little things—holding hands, the smile they'd exchanged only with each other, the way he made her giggle with his Elvis impersonations. "Waiting's been a big part of our lives, hasn't it?"

Entwining his finger with hers, he pulled her ever so gently toward him. "Olivia, thanks to my uncle Seamus and my father's estate, I have money set aside for your business."

Olivia stared into his eyes, nearly losing herself there. "I don't want—"

"Listen to me. Every penny I have will be yours when I die, regardless of whether you want it or not. And look at it this way—my father owes you, doesn't he? Everything I've earned and inherited will eventually go to you and Kyle. So, why not make use of it now?"

She shot him a worried glance. "James, don't talk about dying."

He shrugged. "We all have to die someday."

"Why would you leave me your money? What about your family?"

"You and Kyle *are* my family. The only family I ever really had, other than Julia and Uncle Seamus."

"You must have loved your uncle very much," she said softly. "I'm sorry you lost him."

His smile faltered. "I'd bought the ticket to fly home and find you, when I learned that Uncle Seamus had lung cancer and didn't have long to live."

So he *had* meant to find her. "That must've been a very painful time for you."

"It was. Seamus was more of a father to me than my own. He made my life in Dublin bearable, and he loved me like the son he never had. He told me to go home and look for you. I was ready to do that when he got the bad news, and despite everything, he still wanted me to fly home. I couldn't. He deserved to have family with him when he died."

"I'm glad you were there for him. As much as I would've been so happy to see you, I understand what you were going through. I would've done the same thing."

"After Seamus died, I was afraid too much time had passed, that what we felt for each other didn't exist anymore."

"I guess we both had doubts about our feelings."

"I wish you could've known my uncle," he murmured, touching her cheek, running his fingers lightly over her skin.

Her body tingled at his touch, and she turned her face into his palm. "I wish I could have, too."

"Uncle Seamus never stopped encouraging me to follow my dreams, even when he knew the end was close. And now that I'm here, I want to tell you something. We *deserve* a life together. You've asked me why I didn't tell you the whole truth that night in high school, or why I hadn't since. It's simple. I was afraid."

"AFRAID?" she echoed.

"The meeting with my father was terrifying. I'd never seen him so angry. Not that he didn't often get angry—he did. Julia and I learned very early not to provoke him."

"He was angry at you for dating me?"

The look in her eyes was one of love and compassion, a look he'd lived a lifetime to see again. "Yeah, and when he learned that Julia was part of the deception to keep him and Mom from finding out about you, he threatened to send Julia away to boarding school. He told me that if I defied him, your parents would lose everything."

"What a miserable man he was."

"I went to Dublin, knowing that any move I made toward you could have drastic consequences."

"Your father was even worse than I realized."

"That night in the parking lot, I was afraid to hold you close, or kiss you. I was afraid that if I did, I'd never be able to leave. I couldn't really explain what was happening because I was too shocked and hurt by my father's ultimatum, and too scared of what he'd do."

"Is that why you seemed to be in pain when I touched you?"

Shame flooded his heart. "My father was so angry he hit me."

"Oh, no! I wish I'd known…." Her eyes filled with tears.

"All I could think about was doing whatever he wanted in order to keep you and your family safe. I had this crazy idea that if I did what he asked, he'd relent and let me come home. I was so naive. I didn't know how to stop my father, and had every reason to believe that he'd carry out his threats. I couldn't stand up to him, and I'll have to live with that."

"We both acted in ways we regret. I should've tried harder to find you. I should've taken the plane ticket and gone to London. I would have saved so many people so much grief and pain."

"But if I hadn't let my father rule my life, we would never have been apart. I let you face the aftermath of that day alone when you needed me most," he said, running his fingers lightly over her shoulders.

"I made sure there was no way you could've known about Kyle. I didn't tell anyone, not even Grace. What I did was unfair. I'm sorry."

James saw the need in her eyes, the anxious way she waited for him to make the next move. He took her hands and pulled her to her feet. His arms tight around her, his lips touched her forehead, cruised along her hairline and over the soft skin of her cheeks toward her mouth. His kiss, gentle at first, was urged on by her sudden intake of breath. As he stood holding her in his embrace, the years seemed to slide away as if they'd never happened.

He gave in to the need burning through him, as his hands moved down her back and slid over her bottom. He pressed her against his erection as his tongue swept her mouth.

ALIVE TO HIS touch, Olivia closed her eyes, letting her feelings of lust and longing take over. Her pulse spiked as his hands held her firmly against him, the heat of him wiping everything else from her mind. Reliving what it had once been like for them, she ran her fingers over his neck, feeling the warmth of his skin, the beat of his heart beneath her hand.

Leaning back without breaking the connection between them, James smoothed the hair from her face. "I have a suggestion," he murmured. "Let's take this to your bedroom." Lifting her into his arms, he headed toward the hall leading to the master suite.

"Are you sure?" she said, snuggling into his shoulder.

"How can you doubt it?" he said.

"I was talking about you carrying me in your arms. I've gained a few pounds since the last time you carried me anywhere."

"Not a problem. Besides, this is my version of carrying you over the threshold." He kissed the corner of her mouth.

"Over the threshold? Is this a marriage proposal?"

He held her closer. "Something I should've done years ago."

"It's never too late," she whispered.

"Where am I going? Which bedroom?"

"Two doors down," she said, running her fingers through his dark hair.

Inside her bedroom, she slid to her feet, but refused to take her arms from around his neck.

Surrendering to her need, she pulled him closer and kissed him, her tongue searching for his.

He groaned with pleasure. "The waiting's over," he said, easing her onto the bed. He unbuttoned her cotton shirt and slipped his fingers under it to touch the lace of her bra.

As he undressed her, his hands were steady, his touch so tender, and all she could think of was how long she'd waited. "Please hurry," she moaned.

Her clothes lay scattered around her. She welcomed the cool air against her heated skin. He moved up beside her, his arms circling her as he gazed into her eyes. "I'm not going to rush this."

He touched her collarbone, then her hair, her cheeks, her forehead, and each touch burned brighter than the last.

He kissed her mouth, her eyelids, the hollow of her throat.

She held his head in her hands as his lips slid down over her breasts, circling gently before taking one nipple into his eager mouth, then the other.

She closed her eyes, writhing in the sensation created by his lips. They made love that evening and spent most of the night holding each other.

From that moment forward, they treated each day they shared as something to be savored and cherished.

And in memory of the crazy-in-love teenagers

they'd once been, James and Olivia eloped. They bought a house in Boston and started their new life together.

TWO MONTHS after they returned from their honeymoon, James found himself waiting in Dr. Harris's exam room. Sam Harris had been his family doctor for years, but today's appointment wasn't going quite the way James had hoped. Then again, ever since he'd had rheumatic fever as a child, going to the doctor hadn't been an experience he handled well.

Sam Harris walked in, his white lab coat billowing out behind him. "Well, James, you and I need to talk."

James didn't like the tone of his voice. "I'm listening."

"Why didn't you come to me earlier with your 'indigestion'?"

After he and Olivia had eloped, he'd set up an office in Boston for his own convenience. With all the new technology available, he could work from anywhere these days. The companies in Dublin, under the ownership of Laurel Industries, were running smoothly. And with McElroy Manufacturing sold, James had been studying the possibilities of new investment areas in the hi-tech sector.

He'd been living with a tightness in his chest for

months now, but there never seemed to be enough time in the day to make an appointment. As it was, he'd cancelled an important overseas phone call to be here.

"You know how busy I've been, and with Olivia and me getting married, I didn't have time."

"Did you tell her about your pain?"

"She thinks I have an upset stomach."

"Well, you don't, and you know it." Dr. Harris waved the sheaf of paper in his hands. "I've got the results of all the tests, and you have angina, fairly severe, not to mention the ongoing problem with your mitral valve. You're going to need surgery as soon as I can arrange it."

Not now, not when everything was finally going right in his life. "I don't want Olivia to know about this. Not yet."

"You're going to have to tell her. We have to do the surgery."

"Olivia and I need time to have a normal life first. To get to know each other again, without a crisis getting in the way. Don't do anything until I get back to you," he said firmly.

"Well, I think you should consider the consequences if you don't have this surgery within the next few weeks."

"Meaning I could die of a heart attack."

"You could. Especially with your family

history of heart disease." Dr. Harris folded his arms across his chest. "But if I can't convince you to have the surgery immediately, I want you to do a few things for me."

"I'll do anything to postpone the surgery."

"I can't make any promises, you understand. Your blood pressure is okay, but your cholesterol's too high. I want you on cholesterol medication. You need to see a dietitian and get a low-fat diet going right away. No smoking, no heavy drinking and do moderate exercise, walking and swimming. And call me the minute you have more pain."

"I will."

"The longer you put this off," he warned, "the greater the risk."

"Thanks, Sam. I'll be in touch."

James left the doctor's office, his mind made up. He would postpone telling Olivia about the surgery as long as he could. They had a wonderful life ahead of them, and he meant to enjoy every minute of it. Besides, he didn't feel that bad, only when the pain started. He'd just be extra careful and get more rest.

When he returned to the house, Olivia was waiting for him, hands on her hips and a no-nonsense look in her eyes.

"So, what did the doctor say?"

"He hasn't got all the tests back yet."

Olivia frowned. "That doesn't make any sense. Getting your test results was the whole reason for this appointment."

James did his best to meet her suspicious glance. "This indigestion I have is going to need some form of treatment," he said.

"And what would that be?"

"Sam got me an appointment with a dietitian, and he says I should exercise more."

"Well, you're going to that dietitian if I have to drag you there. No more spicy foods. And we'll cut out coffee. We'll go for a walk every night and…"

Had he convinced her it was only indigestion? He couldn't tell for sure, but he was willing to bluff his way through this, at least until she could trust their happiness was real. Because Olivia's happiness meant everything to him. He would be there for her. And he'd made up his mind that he would meet his son before he went under the knife. What if the surgery didn't go well and he never got the chance? Kyle was on an exchange program in China and he'd be home in a couple of weeks. They'd called to say they'd eloped, but it was impossible to tell whether or not Kyle was pleased.

James had seen the photos of Kyle, and there was a strong family resemblance. He could hardly wait to meet his son, face to face. And he had no intention of doing it from a hospital bed. Besides, the pain wasn't that bad.

CHAPTER FIFTEEN

Two months later

HE AND OLIVIA were waiting for Kyle, who was finally coming home. Kyle hadn't wanted them to meet him at the airport, even though Olivia had threatened all sorts of mayhem. James liked that about his son. Kyle could stand up to his parents, something he hadn't learned to do until it was too late.

"I wonder what Kyle will think?" James asked for the third time that morning.

"We'll find out soon. He should be here any minute," Olivia said, glancing at her watch.

She smiled at James, a tentative smile that made him want to fold her in his arms. "Kyle's looking forward to meeting you. Give him time to get to know you."

"He can have all the time in the world. I've waited this long, I can wait a little longer."

"That's what I love most about you."

"What's that?" he inquired, kissing her fore-head and breathing in her scent. He never tired of touching his wife.

Olivia didn't respond. "I hear a car," she said, her voice infused with excitement as she ducked under his arm and made for the door.

He hung back for a moment. When they came in the door, arm in arm, his breath caught in his throat. Kyle Crawford was the spitting image of his grandfather, Tom McElroy—dark, handsome, with a sense of vitality about him.

"James, I want you to meet Kyle." Olivia's face was alight with love.

"Your mother's told me so much about you," James said, holding out his hand.

Kyle dropped his duffel bag on the hall floor and shook hands with James. "Nice to meet you," he said coolly, his assessing gaze forcing James to suspect that this young man disapproved of his relationship with his mother.

"We're both glad you're here for Thanksgiving. Your mother's been cooking all week," James said, feeling just a bit awkward when he noticed the guarded look Kyle aimed at Olivia.

"Why don't you two chat, while I go check on dinner?" Olivia asked, leading Kyle to the living room.

James knew the first real feeling of love for his

son as he sat across from Kyle. Whenever he'd thought about having a son it had been an abstract thing, a feeling with no basis except in his mind. Until now, he'd only imagined what it would be like to see his only child. Now, here he was—sitting there with reluctance shimmering in his eyes.

"How was China?" James ventured. That seemed safe enough.

"Different, fantastic, frightening, but great," Kyle said, a quick smile softening his face. The same smile James had seen on his father's face when something pleased him.

"What about you? How did you meet my mom?" Kyle asked, leaning forward, curiosity evident in the way he focused on James.

Go slow. Give Kyle time to adjust. "She didn't tell you?"

"No, she didn't. I've only had a couple of phone conversations with her since you two eloped. She's told me about your life together, but not how you met."

"We met in high school."

"That would make it over twenty-seven years ago," Kyle mused, rubbing his jaw.

"Yeah."

"Did you date back then?"

"Sure. You know how it is."

The wariness in Kyle's eyes eased. "I looked

you up on the Internet, and you have business interests in Dublin."

James felt surprise, coupled with admiration for his son. "I'm glad you checked up on me. I want us to be honest with each other."

Kyle settled back against the sofa. "Have you and Mom kept in touch since high school?"

His son obviously wasn't prepared to let the subject drop, and James didn't blame him. "Once in a while."

"Dad says he hasn't met you. He seemed kind of evasive, and I can't figure out why, unless he's protecting Mom for some reason."

"Your mother told me how close you and Alex are." James couldn't think of what else to say.

"Dad and I've had some great times together. He visited me in China, and we went to the Great Wall. What a fantastic place. I'll never forget it." Kyle nervously clasped his hands together.

"I'm glad to hear you had a good time with your dad." And he was, even though he envied Alex and Kyle their closeness.

"I have to ask you something." Kyle's gaze searched James's face.

"Sure," he said, startled by the intensity of the question.

"Were you the reason my mother and father got divorced?"

He didn't want to fumble this, and make Kyle angry. He needed to get to know this young man, who would forever be part of his life, in the hope that someday they, too, would be close.

What if he told his son the truth, and Kyle walked out? What if he didn't, and Kyle walked out anyway? "I've loved your mother for a long time."

"And Mom? Did she feel the same way?"

"I think so, but we didn't do anything about it."

"Because of my dad?"

"Partly, and partly because of a misunderstanding."

"A misunderstanding? About what?"

"About something that happened between us."

Eyes narrowed, Kyle stared at James. "Did the 'something' you're talking about happen twenty-seven years ago?"

The censure in Kyle's eyes said he knew or at least suspected. And it scared James senseless. "Yes."

Kyle's glance moved slowly around the room, coming back to James. "You and I look a whole lot alike, don't you think?"

This was the moment James had been dreading. Kyle was asking, and James wanted to tell him. But he hadn't expected it to be like this. He wanted to be part of his son's life before he told him the truth.

But the truth couldn't wait. "You look very much like my father," he said.

Kyle's expression froze. "So, I was right." With that, he stood up and went to the kitchen, his shoulders stiff.

"Mom, I want to talk to you." Kyle burst into the kitchen where Olivia was preparing their Thanksgiving dinner.

"Sure, honey, what's up?" Olivia asked, sliding the turkey from the oven to the top of the stove.

"I'm planning to have dinner finished before the game, if that's what you're worried about. Did you and James have a chat?"

"We had more than a chat."

"Really? Want to tell me about it?" She glanced at her son and saw the anger in his eyes. "What is it, Kyle?" she asked, trying to control her sudden fear.

"Is the man in our living room my father?"

Oh, no...

"Kyle, sit down." She pointed to the table in the breakfast nook.

"Mom, just tell me. I can take it, I simply want to know if James McElroy is my biological father."

"Kyle, sit down," she said again. "We need to talk," she ordered, going to the kitchen table before her knees gave out.

Kyle followed her, but remained standing. "Tell me the truth," he demanded.

"He is. James McElroy is your father."

Kyle stepped back, his face a mask of shock. "Did Dad know?"

"Alex knew I was expecting you when we got married."

"Why the hell would you keep something like that from me?"

She'd been dreading this moment all her adult life. "It…just happened that way."

"*Just happened that way.* I don't get it."

James appeared at her side and slid into the chair next to hers, his arm resting protectively around her shoulders as he looked up at Kyle.

"I left for Ireland without knowing that your mother was pregnant. She had to fend for herself, and Alex married her."

"To give me a father?" Kyle asked.

Olivia sent her husband a grateful glance before turning her attention back to her son. "Yes, but it was more than that. Alex wanted children and—"

"And I fit the bill. A package deal, is that what you're saying?"

Olivia wished she could take her son in her arms and comfort him, but he wouldn't allow it. The best she could do was try to explain.

"I've loved James most of my life. When I found myself pregnant and alone, I married Alex and decided to keep your birth father a secret. I thought I was protecting you. I did what I believed was right at the time. It wasn't in the end, because I couldn't stop loving James."

She smiled up into James's face, drawing strength from the love she saw in his eyes.

"You're telling me you divorced Dad so you could be with *him*." He gave a cursory nod in James's direction. "You ruined my father's life and you kept me from knowing who my biological father was, kept me from knowing my birth family because you couldn't handle being pregnant without a ring on your finger."

How could she explain something that by today's standards sounded so out-of-date? "It was different back then. Being an unwed mother just wasn't accepted. If I didn't marry someone, and if I couldn't support you, I'd have to give you up for adoption. I couldn't bear to do that. I had no choice but to get married."

"And Dad was a convenience, is that it?"

"No, he was not! Alex and I cared for each other, but not enough to keep the marriage going."

"You're saying you lived all those years with a man you didn't love?" Kyle held her gaze, his angry glare insisting on an answer.

"As I already said, I cared for Alex very much. I'd hoped we could make the marriage work. I was trying to do the right thing by providing you with a home and family."

Kyle shoved his fingers through his dark hair. "That man you claim not to love is my father. And *I* love him, even if you never did."

Olivia met his contemptuous eyes. "Even though I never stopping loving James, Alex and I had a good relationship. We still do. I owe him so much."

"Except your love, right, Mom?"

Her shoulders tensed against the pain of Kyle's words. "I know it must seem hypocritical to you, but you would've been labeled illegitimate and looked down on by others in the community. I couldn't let that happen."

"So, you married someone you didn't love."

"Kyle, we don't choose who to love." How would she ever make him understand? "I'm handling this really badly, aren't I?"

"I'm not something to be handled, Mom. I'm your son, and I deserved the truth. But your love for *him*—" he tossed a dismissive glance James's way "meant more to you than telling me the truth. Or being fair to Dad."

"I was young and inexperienced. There was no one to turn to, except Alex."

"He was good to you, and you divorced him. And married a man who didn't care enough to be my father."

"That's not true! For one thing, the divorce was a mutual decision. For another, James didn't know about you until recently. I married Alex, and I made a mistake by not telling James about you—a mistake I deeply regret."

"That's because you were thinking about yourself, Mom, not about me or my father."

"Kyle, you're not being rational," James interjected. "Your mother's trying to tell you how it was back then, how hard her choices were."

Kyle moved away from the table, his scornful eyes sweeping them both. "So this is how it's going to be. Not only did you divorce my father, but now you want me to accept this man in his place."

Terrified by her son's anger and accusations, Olivia stood up and went to him. "Kyle, I'm sorry you're upset. I wish we'd done this differently. But if you'll just take some time to think about this, you'll see things a little more clearly."

Ignoring his mother's plea, Kyle turned on James. "I don't want to see you again. My mother loves you—I can see it in her face and how she behaves around you. But I don't want you in my life."

"Please, Kyle, don't do this! You have to give us a chance to explain. Don't do something you'll regret." Olivia clutched Kyle's arm.

Kyle yanked his arm away and continued to stare at James.

"You could've claimed me a lifetime ago, and

you didn't. You're not my father, except by blood, and blood doesn't mean anything. I ought to know."

His face flushed and his eyes glittering with unshed tears, Kyle backed out of the kitchen. "Happy Thanksgiving, Mom."

The slamming of the front door reverberated through the house.

CHAPTER SIXTEEN

SEVERAL MONTHS LATER, James stood gazing up at the towering facade of the house that had once been home. He and Olivia had driven from Boston to Frampton to visit his mother.

They'd worried about Kyle, wondered whether he could be convinced to come back, to talk with them, but after a few weeks, they'd decided to let him heal his anger and the sense of treachery he felt.

Finding out that he was a father, and fumbling his first contact with Kyle, made James want to understand more about his own parents. Had he misunderstood their motives, much like Kyle had misunderstood his and Olivia's?

He didn't think so, but seeing his mother might show him, one way or another. He wanted her to know about his son, too, a son who might help him feel closer to his surviving parent.

As he looked up at the window in his childhood room, he wondered why he'd been so intimidated by this place. Or was it simply the two people who had inhabited the dark rooms and oppressively ornate spaces?

When he'd lived at home, his parents had employed a gardener, a cook and a chauffeur. Since his father's death, his mother stayed in the house with the assistance of her old chauffeur and cook.

Susan McElroy had spurned any interest he showed in her well-being, and even more so after he and Olivia were married. Elopement was not in his mother's vocabulary.

"Are you sure this is a good idea?" Olivia asked, sliding her arm around his waist, reassuring him. "We could put this off until later. Your mother isn't going to be happy regardless of when we tell her."

"But she has to be told about Kyle, and I don't want her finding out from someone else."

"You're right," Olivia said with a sigh.

"You don't have to come with me if you don't want to."

"Don't go all tough and macho on me. We did this together, and we'll tell her together."

"Then let's do it." He grinned down at Olivia, basking in her smile.

They walked arm in arm up the walkway to the large, baroquely carved front door and rang the bell. The door opened smoothly, and Lionel, the chauffeur, let his glance skip over Olivia to James. "Please come in, sir. Your mother's expecting *you*."

He'd managed to run a successful multinational company, he thought wryly, and yet he still put up with this kind of arrogance from his mother's poor excuse for staff. He and his lawyers and accountants looked after her financial affairs, but she insisted on employing this nasty old bastard.

"If I ever darken this door again and you behave as rudely to my wife as you just did, I will have you fired."

Lionel's ruddy cheeks grew redder as he turned to Olivia. "I apologize, ma'am."

"Some things never change. I'm still invisible to the upper classes, even to their hired help," Olivia said sardonically.

"Not to worry, this is absolutely the last time you'll have to endure that sort of treatment."

Ignoring the man's directions to follow him to the den, James and Olivia walked along the hall toward the formal living room.

"Tell my mother we'll wait in here," he said, saving his smile for his wife.

The first thought he had as he entered the huge room was how stagnant it seemed. How unchanged. The light still struggled to peek through the heavy drapery drawn against the afternoon sun. The massive fireplace still held sway in the room, like some relic from a bygone era. The inlaid teak ceiling still glowered at those who stood beneath it.

The silence of the house spoke of loneliness and dread, of a life not really lived…and yet his mother always claimed to be perfectly happy here.

Had *he* been happy here? Sometimes.

Had he ever felt loved here? He wasn't sure.

He studied the somber lines of the room as he and Olivia sat on the tapestry-covered love seat, waiting for his mother. And the longer he waited, the more certain he was that this couldn't be anybody's idea of living.

Especially not his. He wanted light, warmth and laughter. Life was meant to be enjoyed, not buried behind the archaic walls of a place like this.

He couldn't remember ever hearing his parents laugh or joke with each other. His early mornings in this house had consisted of getting dressed, getting breakfast and getting out of the house without disturbing his father's routine.

Why hadn't he realized before this just how cold and impersonal his life had been as a child? He'd had all the material things money could buy. But he'd never been allowed to bring anyone home from school or have a friend stay overnight.

He supposed that by most people's standards he was very fortunate. Yet he'd seldom felt the excitement and lightheartedness he'd experienced with Olivia. He saw the anxious lines around her mouth. "Don't worry. This'll be over soon."

"Why does this place make me feel like I'm at the dentist's?" she muttered.

James chuckled. "Or maybe a funeral home."

"You feel this way about it, too? The house you grew up in?"

"Yeah, I do." He leaned over and kissed her, tightening his arms around her shoulders and pulling her to him. He gloried in the scent of her, the feel of her body hugging his—

The murmur of silk intruded. He smiled at Olivia's startled face before glancing at his mother.

"Well, I see I've interrupted you," his mother said.

"Not at all," Olivia murmured politely, smoothing her hair, her glance swerving from James to his mother.

"Good afternoon, Mother," he said, rising to kiss her rouged cheek.

"Good afternoon, son," she said, her voice like steel, her body stiff in his embrace.

He stepped away from her. "Mom, I don't think you've met my wife, Olivia."

"She and I spoke on the phone years ago." Susan McElroy stared at Olivia as she rose from the love seat.

"Yes, we did. You refused to tell me how to reach James."

"And I'd do it again, my dear," his mother said, the words lacking her usual cultured inflection.

"Mom, don't talk to my wife that way." James stretched out his hand to Olivia and drew her close.

With a lift of her shoulders, Susan McElroy turned away.

"There's not a chance in hell that your mother will ever accept me," she whispered to James.

Susan McElroy moved to a straight-backed chair at one end of the love seat, and sat down, her eyes hard. "I didn't mean to offend you, Olivia. I was merely stating my position." Her fingers gripped the carved arms of the chair.

His mother's coldness made him wish he could just walk out the door. "Mom, we have some news."

"That you eloped." She spat out the word. "No self-respecting couple would elope."

He was a grown man, and still he felt his mother's disapproval like a blow. Why was he wasting his time here?

"Our elopement is not your concern, Mother," he said calmly. "We don't need to hear any more of your criticism." He glanced at Olivia. "Let's go."

She shook her head, her gaze steady on the older woman as she held James's arm. "Your mother may never change her mind about us and our life, but she's not going to run me out of here before we say what we came to say."

He resisted the urge to kiss her. "You're right. My mother's not making our decisions."

He turned back to his mother. "Whether you approve of our marriage or not, we want you to know how happy we are and how—"

"So, you think you know what happiness is?" the older woman broke in.

Something resembling vulnerability flashed in his mother's eyes as she stared at Olivia. Loneliness lurked in her guarded expression. But James blocked the rush of pity he felt for his mother. "Yes, we know what happiness is. We have a wonderful life ahead of us, and we'd like you to share in it—if you're willing to change your attitude."

"It's not *my* attitude that's the problem," Susan snapped.

Ignoring her anger, James knelt down and took his mother's bony hand in his. "We have a son."

"A son. Just like that." She looked from James to Olivia. "You have a son. Where is he?" she asked, her hands vibrating under his touch.

"His name is Kyle."

Susan's face was as stiff as her posture. "How old is he?"

"He's twenty-seven, nearly twenty-eight."

"He couldn't be! You were in Ireland," his mother said, quickly, her eyes triumphant.

"Mom, Olivia was pregnant when I left for Ireland."

His mother's face went white; her sudden

intake of breath accompanied the jabbing motion of her hands as she reached for James. "Tell me it isn't true."

"But it is. I'm a father, and you're a grandmother."

"You're sure he's your son?" she hissed.

Shocked at her hateful words, James let go of his mother's hand and stepped back. "Apologize to Olivia or I'll walk out of here and never come back."

His mother drew in another deep breath, her gaze furtive. "I'm sorry. That remark was uncalled for," she mumbled, glancing up at Olivia.

"Apology accepted," Olivia said as graciously as she could.

James grabbed Olivia's hand, his heart pounding with anger.

"Olivia, James, I want to see my grandson." Susan McElroy stood with difficulty, her eyes blinking to hold back…tears? "My only grandchild," she whispered.

"We'll bring him to see you when he comes back."

"Back? Where is he? Still in school somewhere?"

James nodded. "He's finishing his doctorate and teaching part-time."

"Then bring him home to visit. I want to see my grandson," she demanded again.

"We can't," Olivia said.

"And why not?" She shot the words at Olivia.

"Because Kyle has had some difficulty adjusting to his new circumstances."

"What do you mean?"

"Kyle's still getting used to the idea that his father is James and not Alex, my first husband," Olivia said.

His mother rounded on him. "How could you let your life get so out of control? Where's your sense of right and wrong? You had a—" her lips worked "—relationship with Olivia, you got her pregnant, and now you have a son who obviously doesn't want you in his life. When will you ever learn?"

James held his anger in check, reminding himself that his mother was a lonely old woman. "Mom, Kyle will get over this. He's a smart young man."

"Unlike his father."

Like bricks thrown against the wall, the words broke and crashed at his feet. In one resounding moment of truth, he saw that his mother's love wasn't absolute; it was conditional on his complying with what she wanted and what she believed.

Everything in her life was built on appearances—how people were supposed to act, not how they really felt. Any genuine feeling she had was frozen inside her implacable heart. Why had he struggled to meet her lofty expectations, to be the hard-nosed businessman she and his father had wanted? It seemed so pointless now.

He'd traded his happiness for their approval, an approval that was as conditional as the love they offered.

"If you meant what you just said, we have nothing left to discuss."

His mother gave him a defiant glare.

"Come on, Olivia, we're out of here." He took her hand and they walked to the door.

He didn't look back, and his mother uttered not a word.

Outside he filled his lungs with fresh, clean air. "How could I have been so stupid? All these years…and all the times I thought she cared."

Olivia hugged him, her hands framing his face as she gazed into his eyes. "James, don't think about what went on in there. Your mother's a very unhappy woman who couldn't possibly understand what we feel for each other."

"You're telling me," he said, kissing her lips and feeling a whole lot better for it.

"I'm glad you stood up to her. Let's get away from all this and go somewhere pleasant," she said.

The love in her eyes wiped away the anger brewing in him. "I want to tell you what I realized only a few minutes ago."

"And that would be?" she asked, cuddling closer.

"I could never be like that."

"Not in a million years," she confirmed.

"I love you and Kyle without condition. I wouldn't want to live my life not knowing how it feels to love someone more than you love yourself."

"So, that's how it is?" she asked, a smile on her lips, her eyes misting with happy tears.

"That's how it is."

Thankful for her touch and the way she made him feel, he led her down the steps toward the car.

AND DESPITE everything, they'd been happy during the years that followed, Olivia mused as she walked out of James's hospital room and started down the corridor.

After that heartbreaking visit with James's mother, Olivia had reconciled herself to the idea that she and James would be all the family they had, other than her parents. Sure, there were close to his sister, who was very busy building her career, but other than Julia, James had no family left.

There was Kyle. After all this time, Olivia could still see the anger in Kyle's eyes, the way he hadn't looked back as he strode down the hall and out of their lives.

No matter when she dialed his number in Scotland, where he was doing postdoctoral work in anthropology, she got his voice mail. She'd made sure his bank accounts were kept open, and periodically she'd see from the bank statement that he'd taken money out.

She'd talked to Alex several times about Kyle, explaining her predicament over Kyle's behavior. He was very sympathetic. He told her Kyle hadn't been to see him, but he did get the occasional phone call in which he seemed okay. And Alex, being his usual kind self, reassured her that if Kyle did show up, he'd encourage their son to go and see her and James.

Alex sounded happy with his life, and busy with his dealerships. He was making plans to retire, and wondered out loud if Kyle might be convinced to go into the business. But best of all, in the last call she'd made to him, he told her that he'd met a woman his age whose company he enjoyed. She teased him about being finished with playing the field and he laughed.

For two years they'd waited and hoped that Kyle would call, get in touch with them in some way. Then, about a month after 9/11, he showed up.

Olivia had been too happy to see him to ask many questions. Kyle had apologized to her, but said little to James, and a week later he was gone again. One day he called her from Europe, where he'd gotten a job with a ski equipment company, something to do with chairlifts. Why he'd chosen to leave his field of anthropology, she didn't know, and Kyle didn't explain.

Funny how life never turns out the way anyone expects, she mused as she dialed Kyle's number for the umpteenth time. Unwilling to leave yet another message on his voice mail, she was about to hang up when she heard his voice.

"Oh, thank God, you're there," she said, gripping the phone for support.

"I got stranded by an avalanche, and couldn't pick up my messages. I just got back to the office. What happened?"

Worried about how Kyle would respond, she plunged forward. "James has had heart surgery, and he's not doing very well. I need you here with me."

There was such a long pause that Olivia feared the connection had been broken. "Kyle—"

"Please don't worry, Mom. I'm coming home."

Her son's words sent waves of relief surging through her. She missed him so much, and her guilt over how she'd handled everything had left her with a deep need to recover all the time they'd lost. She knew it wasn't possible, but it didn't keep her from wishing. "Kyle, it's so good to hear your voice."

"I've booked a flight for tomorrow morning, and I'll go straight from the airport to the hospital."

"Kyle, I can't wait to see you. And James, too. He's fought so hard…."

"I know, Mom, I know…I love you, Mom."

"I love you, too. So much."

An hour later

"ARE YOU OKAY?" Julia asked, coming along the hospital corridor toward Olivia, her sunglasses nestled in her hair.

"I can hardly believe it," she said, turning to her sister-in-law. "Kyle's on his way home!"

"That's great. When?"

"Tomorrow." Olivia wasn't sure of the time difference, and it didn't matter.

"Have you told James?"

"No, I'm going to do that now."

Behind Julia, Olivia spotted her mother walking toward her, a questioning look on her face.

"Hi, Mom." She gave her a grateful hug.

"Olivia, dear, I'm going to take you home for a break. You need to get away from this place for a while."

"I will, just as soon as I talk to James about Kyle."

"Kyle's coming home, is he?" Tears glistened in her mother's eyes.

"Yeah, Mom, he's coming home."

Her mother kissed her on the cheek. "You go in and see James. Tell him your good news."

"We'll wait right here for you," Julia said, a smile of happiness lifting the strain from her face.

AFTER WHAT felt like the longest wait so far, Olivia was allowed back into James's room. His bed was raised a bit, and her husband appeared much better to her weary eyes.

"Hi, there, beautiful. I thought the warden was never going to let you back in," he said, referring to the nurse. Was she imagining it, or was his voice a little stronger than before?

Feeling hopeful for the first time, Olivia kissed his cheek, the whiskers scratching her lips. "You look like a pirate, minus the eye patch," she teased, gently stroking his forehead.

"As long as I'm your favorite pirate," he said, giving her a grin she hadn't seen for days.

"I've got great news, honey. Kyle called and he's coming home. He wants to see you." She squeezed his hand. "He says he's sorry—"

A muscle jumped in his jaw, and tears slid unchecked down his cheeks. "How soon will he be here?"

If she'd ever needed proof of his love for Kyle, she had only to look at her husband's face. "Oh, darling, he said he's leaving tomorrow morning. He'll come right here from the airport."

She wiped the tears staining his cheeks, love for

him making her fingers tremble where they touched his skin.

"I've been wishing I could see him all morning," James said, his voice drenched with feeling.

"And all this time I figured you were asleep," she chided gently.

"Well, maybe I dreamed it—so many pleasant thoughts about how he'd come back and stay with us for a while. I need to see him."

"We both do."

"I've missed every part of his life. That's what I've been thinking about this last while—all the wonderful times we could've had together. I regret not knowing him as a child."

"I wish you'd been with us," she said, pressing a cool facecloth to his forehead.

"And I want him here so he'll be able to look after you until I take over again," he said, a twinkle in his eye.

"Will you please not worry about me," she scolded.

"You might as well tell me not to breathe."

Not trusting her voice, she nodded her head.

"I want to go home with you," James said.

"You will very soon."

"I want us to have one of those dinner parties you love to host. I want to see the smile in your eyes when you open the door to your friends."

"You'll have it all, I promise. We'll have the best and biggest party yet, when you're up to it."

He massaged the palm of her hand. "I want our family together, the three of us."

CHAPTER SEVENTEEN

Three Years before the surgery

"Ouch!" Olivia sucked her burned finger.

"You need any help?" James asked, standing at the door of the kitchen.

"No, I just forgot the pan was hot, that's all."

"And you a renowned restaurateur, your restaurants franchised across the country. Don't let your adoring public find out," he teased, taking her hand in his and kissing each finger.

A warm flush worked its way through her body. In the time they'd been together, she'd been incapable of resisting him.

"I have a surprise for you."

"Another restaurant franchise signed?"

"Nothing that mundane. It's something very special, something you'll love."

"What would that be, and where are you hiding it?" Olivia patted the breast pocket of his suit jacket.

"Hey, lady, don't get fresh. On second thought—"

He lifted his arms and leered at her. "Be my guest. But whatever you start, we'll have to finish, right here and now in this kitchen." He kissed her nose. "That's a promise."

"I'm going to ignore that comment," she said, running her fingers over his chest, checking the inside pocket of his jacket as she did so. James's last surprise, two tickets to Italy, had been in the pocket of his shirt.

On Valentine's Day he'd walked into the kitchen, just as he'd done this time, and handed her a set of Italian language tapes.

"It was easier last time." She slipped two fingers into the pocket of his cotton shirt. "It's got to be here *somewhere.*"

"Lower, honey, you gotta go lower," he groaned.

"Want me to frisk you? I can do it, you know."

"I'll assume the position, Officer." He stepped back, raised his arms higher and spread his legs. "In the name of making my wife happy." A small grimace crossed his face.

"Did that hurt?" she asked as she watched him lower his arms.

"Not a bit." He gazed at the ceiling, a smile back on his face.

"Just remember you asked for this." She gave

him a quick kiss before reaching into his pants pocket and pulling out an envelope. "So, what have we here?" she asked.

She opened the envelope, tearing it in her eagerness, and unfolded the document tucked inside. "It's a deed. I don't understand. A deed to what?" She stared at him.

"Read it," he said, holding her tight to his side. "It's for us. Land to build our house on."

Olivia unfolded the crisp sheets of paper and began to read. "You bought land in Ireland?"

"I did. Remember that day at the cottage, when you and I were trying to stay out of each other's arms?"

"Vaguely…"

He kissed her hard on the lips. "Liar."

She returned his kiss. "Guilty."

"Stop trying to distract me," he warned, a smile crinkling the corners of his eyes.

"Back to business and the land in Ireland," she said, giving him a playful jab. "I remember telling you that day that I'd done some reading on Ireland. Actually I took every book out of the Bar Harbor Library and read them from cover to cover."

"And this is what you get for your efforts. I bought a piece of land, and I've hired an architect to design the house of our dreams. What do you say?"

Speechless, she smiled at her husband, her gaze

taking in the tiny grooves that bracketed his mouth, to the way his dark lashes framed his eyes.

"I'm the luckiest woman alive to have you," she murmured.

"So, we'll head for Ireland just as soon as this dinner party is over tonight."

"Not tonight! I have to pack."

"Okay, not tonight, but bright and early tomorrow morning, we'll be winging our way to Ireland, land of the shamrock, and our home away from home for as long as it pleases you."

He wrapped his arms around her, his mouth coming down on hers, his kiss hot and demanding.

She kissed him back while her hands played over his muscled chest, taking pleasure in his sudden intake of breath. Her husband was still in great shape, despite being nearly fifty-five.

He palmed her breasts. "Don't you dare," she whispered, doing her best to act as if she could resist him.

"Dare what?"

"I know what you're up to, James McElroy, and it's not going to work."

"How do you know? I'm not done yet," he said, pulling her against him, his breath on her face, his hands locked around her waist as he kissed her again.

It was a simple kiss, filled with promise—a

promise he always kept. His taste, the warmth of his body and the strength of his hands drew her closer.

"I hope you never tell our neighbors how we spend our spare time," she said.

Splaying his hands in her hair, he chuckled. "As a matter of interest, Millie Rayworth asked me just the other day, and I told her in very graphic detail exactly what we do when we're home alone."

"You did not! Millie would've been at my office in record time to find out if you were telling the truth."

"Uh-uh. Millie was so shocked she's still recovering."

"How can you say that about my friend?"

"Easy. She wanted details. So I told her about all our trysts—in the laundry room, the office, the storage room in the basement. Oh, she liked that one," he said his eyes alight with mischief. "She was taking notes."

She kissed his lips. "You did not tell Millie any such thing and she wouldn't be taking notes." She gave him a wry smile. "I know for a fact that they'd be wasted on that couch potato she lives with—but it's a great story."

"Should we try some of the less conventional areas of the house, so we can *really* report back on our experiences?"

"Not unless you want Millie and Joe to walk in on us, and that's probably more graphic than you intended. They're supposed to be here in about—" she glanced at the clock over the sink "—twenty minutes!"

"Come on." He took her by the arm and led her out of the kitchen.

"What about the laundry room? Want to give it a try?" he asked, grinning the wide grin Olivia adored.

"What if I said yes?"

He danced her around in a circle, his arms holding her in a fervent embrace. "Your decision, Madame Executive."

"Not this time. We might accidentally hit a button on the washer and flood the place."

"Excuses, excuses... After you," he said, pointing to the stairs that led to their bedroom. "It's not the laundry room, but it'll have to do."

AND SO it went in their lives. The passion never slackened, and their love for each other shone brighter with each passing day.

It was disheartening to realize that they were beyond the point of having more children, but they'd accepted the reality. They were so glad to be together, and nothing made them happier than to spend hours alone in each other's company.

The only darkness in their otherwise happy

life was Kyle, who sternly refused any invitation to visit them. Olivia and James never stopped trying to convince him to come home, and never gave up hope that one day their son would be with them.

James saw so much of his father in Kyle, and worried that his stubbornness might end up having the same disastrous effect on Olivia's life that his father's stubbornness had had on his.

"Here's hoping history doesn't repeat itself," he sighed, happy to be in Ireland.

"History? You mean this place?" Olivia glanced around at the rolling green fields surrounding the path they'd taken.

"No, not this particular place. The only history here is the history of you and me." He held her hand in his, feeling her warmth as he so often did when they were walking on their property.

They'd built a large two-story Georgian-style house with a solarium and greenhouse. Every bit of wood, stone and mortar had been lovingly assembled by them as they worked month after month to make their dream house a reality.

"The history of you and me—I like that," she said, squinting up at him, in the bright spring sunlight.

"I do, too. I never imagined that a house could hold such happiness, but maybe it's the fact of building the house from scratch that makes it so special."

"No, I really believe this place is enchanted," Olivia said contentedly as she linked arms with James.

"What would you think of moving here permanently?"

"I don't know. Building this place from the ground up has been wonderful, but to live here full-time...I don't know."

"You still want to be home in case Kyle decides to return, is that it?"

"Partly, and also I miss the restaurant. I worked so hard to make it a success and now, when it's going well, it would be nice to enjoy it."

"Remember when I told you I thought you'd someday change the world?"

She'd never forgotten his words back in high school, and it warmed her heart to think that he hadn't, either. "Franchising is hardly changing the world."

"Ah, but in your own way you *did*. You've given families an affordable dining experience with a touch of class."

"I hadn't thought of it that way."

"Speaking of thoughts, have you given any more to the buyout offer Dayton Foods made you?"

"No, but I'll wait and see. If they're interested,

there might be others who are, as well." She grinned at him. "Anytime you feel like helping out in the negotiations, please do."

"No, it's your business."

"That's one of the things I love about you. You let me be whatever I want."

"You're too smart and energetic to spend your life waiting on me." He tucked her arm close to his body. "Although I have to say that having you lounge around the house, ready to do my bidding, does have a certain appeal."

"Don't get your hopes up."

He laughed. "Okay, but how about if we make plans to have Christmas here, in this house, and find a way to get Kyle to join us?"

"I'd love that. Do you think it's possible?" Her voice caught.

He'd give anything to remove that anxious expression from her face. "Why not? We could have lots of fun. We'll make our own tree ornaments, string popcorn, maybe have the neighbors over for dinner. I'll get it organized."

They walked along the hedgerow leading up the drive, thinking their own thoughts. James cherished these quiet times, times when their silence communicated more clearly than words. "Are you happy?" he asked, knowing the answer but loving her response.

"You know I am." She glanced up at him, her face suffused with joy.

"And this house?"

"My favorite place in the world."

James closed his eyes and soaked in the feeling of her body next to his as they walked together, their strides matching. He'd awakened this morning with a heavy sensation in his chest that wouldn't go away, and for the past few hours he'd had a strange tingling down his left arm. The last time he'd seen Dr. Harris, the doctor had warned him that nothing had changed; in fact, his heart was getting progressively worse. Sam had been very insistent that James have the surgery as soon as possible.

But nothing in this world would change James's mind. After the years wasted without Olivia, he'd rather die in her arms, living the life they'd chosen, than relinquish a moment of happiness with her.

"Oh, by the way. Mom called, and she's having a surprise eightieth birthday party for Dad. She'd like us to be there."

"With bells on," he said, stopping to kiss her.

She kissed him back. "Have I mentioned lately that I love you?" she whispered.

He ran his fingers along the V of her sweater, watching the way her eyes widened with pleasure when he touched her. "Yes, I believe you did. And it's actually rumored that I love you, too," he said, playing along.

As so many times before, James offered thanks to whatever fates might be responsible for his good fortune in finding his way back to the one woman he'd ever loved.

Somehow, despite his ineptness and poor judgment, Olivia was part of his life again.

THEY ARRIVED in Frampton for the birthday party, and the happiness between Olivia's parents was a reminder of how married life could be. Her father insisted on breaking out cigars for the occasion.

"You don't mind if I have one, do you?" James asked.

Olivia wrinkled her nose. "As long as you throw your clothes in the wash when you come back into the house."

He pulled her into his lap. "Don't like the aroma of a good cigar?" he half growled.

"You could always refuse Dad's offer."

He waggled his eyebrows at her. "And ruin his birthday? After all, I'm the only son-in-law he has, a poor excuse for one though I might be."

"Not true, but I will tell you I like the way you smell—uncluttered by cigar smoke." She kissed the bridge of his nose.

"Are you coming on to me?" he asked, kissing her in return.

"Can you two take your hands off each other long enough for James to propose a toast?" Grace asked, her laughter forced.

"Let me get back to you on that," James replied, his gaze never leaving his wife's face.

"You'd better do what the woman says," Olivia whispered in his ear.

"Or live to pay for it, right?" he whispered back.

Feeling happy and content, Olivia watched the men as they went out to the patio, each holding a cigar and looking ridiculously pleased.

"Are we ready for the gagging and spewing?" Grace commented, sitting beside Olivia.

"Don't let them know you think so little of their smoking efforts," Olivia warned good-humouredly.

"Not likely. But I'm worried about James. When did he start hunching his shoulders like that?"

Olivia glanced at James's back as he strolled out. She hadn't noticed anything.... "He's not hunching his shoulders. What do you mean?"

"Earlier, when we sat at dinner. The way he moves as if he's guarding against some sort of pain.... I haven't seen either of you in months, but I'm sure he wasn't like that when the two of you left for Ireland."

"James has had indigestion for years."

Grace cocked one eyebrow. "You're positive?"

Olivia remembered the day he'd raised his arms to tease her about frisking him. "The only thing I've seen that was a little off was the way he raised his arms over his head one day, that's all."

"My dad had a coronary and he couldn't lift his arms without pain," Grace said.

LATER THAT evening when they were getting ready for bed, Olivia couldn't help watching the way her husband moved about the bedroom. Was Grace right? Did James have a heart problem?

He'd had a terrible coughing spasm after the cigar-smoking episode, and his color had been pale ever since.

"When did you last see Dr. Harris?"

"Oh, a couple of months ago. Before we went to Ireland."

James was acting far too casual. "What did he say? What about your stomach, your indigestion?"

"He says I'm doing fine on the medication," James said, keeping his back to her while he fiddled with something in the armoire.

"James, where is that medication? I want to see it."

Ever so slowly, he turned to face her, a sheepish look on his face. "Olivia, please don't worry about me. I'm fine."

Why hadn't she pushed him about this before? "I'll decide that for myself. Tell me about your medication."

James came around the bed, and pulled her down beside him. "Olivia, I haven't told you the whole story. But before I do, I want to explain why I didn't."

"James, what is it?"

He took her hand in his, fingers caressing her palm, an old move of his that always made her knees quake. "Dr. Harris says I have some blocked arteries around my heart."

"Blocked arteries? That's serious! People have heart attacks from blocked arteries. Has the doctor suggested surgery?"

"Yes, he has." James tucked a strand of her hair behind her ear, his gaze imploring her to understand.

She wanted to curl up in his arms and block out his words. "When?"

"When I agree to it."

"And why haven't you agreed to it?"

He shrugged. "Because we've had so much going on, and because I wasn't willing to interrupt our lives."

Olivia fought the fear rising in her throat. If anything happened to him… "James, how could you postpone this surgery?"

"I just wanted us to be happy. I wanted you to know the kind of life we'd always planned together."

"James, I *have* the life I want. You and I are together. That's all I've ever wanted." He'd spent all those days in Ireland with her, supervising the construction of their new home, and never once said a word to her. She wanted to be angry with him, and in a way she was, but she couldn't deny the raw love and longing she saw in his eyes.

But there was something else going on; something in his eyes had changed. "You've been having bouts of pain all along, haven't you? And they're getting worse."

He nodded slowly.

She took his face in her hands. "You will call Dr. Harris tomorrow, and you will tell him you want the surgery as soon as he can schedule it."

LATER THAT NIGHT, Olivia awoke to the sound of breaking glass. "James! Is someone downstairs?"

Hearing no response, her hands moved over the empty space beside her. "James?"

A soft groan came from the floor next to his armoire. "James!" she cried, scrambling down and kneeling beside him, barely able to hear over the pounding of her heart.

"Help me up, Olivia," he said, holding his arm out to her.

She helped him up onto the bed and switched on the lamp. In the muted light, his forehead shone with perspiration. "You're sweating."

"Olivia, if anything happens to me, I want you—" His face contorted in pain, and he closed his eyes. "I want you to call Kyle."

"Nothing's going to happen. Nothing," she murmured, fighting the tide of panic. Willing herself to stay calm, she took his hand, stroking his cheek as she tried to calm him. "Where's the pain?"

He glanced at her, his blue-tinged lips in a grimace. "In my chest, up into my throat," he gasped. "Call an ambulance."

CHAPTER EIGHTEEN

OLIVIA STARED out the window of the waiting room, aware of how her life had changed since her husband's surgery. She never closed her eyes without seeing James lying in pain on the floor.

She hadn't considered what their life would be like once he was well enough to go home. He'd said he'd like to go back to Ireland and recuperate there, and she was more than prepared to take him, as long as Dr. Crealock and Dr. Harris gave their approval.

In the meantime she'd stayed by his bedside when the nurses allowed it while she waited for Kyle, whose flight from Paris should have landed by now.

"Here you are," Julia said, her peach-colored jacket flowing around her as she strolled into the waiting room. "There's a call at the nursing station for you."

"Is it Kyle?"

"Sorry. It's my mom."

Olivia raised her eyebrows. "What does she want?"

"I don't know."

Olivia went to the desk and took the phone. "Olivia, I'm not well enough to come to the hospital today," her mother-in-law said, her voice remarkably gentle.

"I understand how hard this is for you."

"And you, no doubt. I was wondering if there's any chance James could take a call in his room?"

"He's still too sick for that," Olivia answered.

"I need to talk to him about an urgent matter."

How typical of her mother-in-law to put what *she* needed first. "I'll tell him you'd like to talk to him. Will that do?"

"I guess it will have to."

The conversation ended soon after that, and Olivia settled in to wait for her son.

"Mom tells me that you and James paid her a visit to tell her about Kyle," Julia said.

"Did she tell you how badly she behaved?"

Julia nodded. "She did, actually, and she says she's really sorry."

Olivia doubted that very much, but said nothing. She liked Julia and didn't see any point in saying things that would make her feel she had to defend her mother. Besides, Olivia didn't want to talk about Susan McElroy. Words wouldn't change the woman. "Why don't we go down to the cafeteria and have a bite to eat?"

"If you feel like eating, James must be improving."

AFTER THEY came back from the cafeteria, Olivia walked the floor, waiting for Kyle to arrive; her feelings flipping from one extreme—the fear that Kyle might be his usual withdrawn self around James—to the other—joy that he was willing to spend time with his father.

During the long wait, she'd decided one thing. If Kyle arrived unwilling to accept her husband as his father, she was prepared to stop trying. Kyle had been estranged from them for years, a reaction she'd never imagined her son capable of, but one she could no longer tolerate.

She and James had paid a high price for their happiness, and Kyle had to acknowledge that.

She was about to go back into James's room when she saw a tall, dark-haired man striding down the corridor. The way he held his body was so sweetly familiar to her. "Kyle!" she cried, running toward him, arms open, her heart lifting in happiness.

"Mom, it's great to see you," he said, giving her a smile as he dropped his bag and hugged her close.

Kyle's smile was so much like his father's. "Are you all right?"

"Tired, but fine. I told you we were delayed by an avalanche? We dug for hours to get two of my crew out."

She nodded. "I'm just glad you're okay."

"Me, too."

"Your father's waiting for you."

"How is he?"

He hadn't asked to see James, only how he was. She steeled herself for disappointment. "Holding his own at the moment, but it's been touch and go. He had a heart attack four days ago. I was with him when it happened. I got him to the hospital by ambulance—" A breathless feeling stopping her words.

"Mom, I'm glad to be here, and sorry for all the trouble I've caused you and my dad."

Olivia had waited years for these words. Gulping back the tears, she touched her son's shoulder. "It's all right now. You're here and your father's anxious to see you."

"Before we go in, I want to talk to you."

Oh, no. "What is it?"

"I don't know how to say what needs to be said. I've been a complete idiot, and I haven't got a clue why you and James ever put up with me."

"We love you, Kyle," she said simply.

"I should know that by now, shouldn't I?" he

said wryly. "It's funny how it took an avalanche to make me see what really matters. I've been a selfish SOB, but that's going to change."

"You don't know how good it makes me feel to hear you say that."

"I learned something last week."

Olivia looked anxiously into her son's face. "What?"

"Let's sit down for a minute." Kyle led her to a quiet corner of the waiting room. "I hadn't gotten your message because I got trapped behind that avalanche, and it took days for the rescuers to get to us. While we were stranded, I had a chance to think about what I've been doing. I decided that when I got out, I'd do something positive with my life, make real plans for my future. Most important, though, I had time to think about you and James—my father—and how hard your lives must have been when you were separated from each other."

"But we got through it, Kyle. We all have problems. Some we overcome and some we don't."

"No kidding. My problem is that I only saw what happened from the perspective of a privileged child. You and Alex always showed me so much love and caring, and I took that for granted."

"And now?"

"Now? I talked to Alex on my way here in the

cab. I spilled my guts to him about everything." Kyle grinned, shaking his head wryly. "He told me to get a life, that you and James deserved my understanding and love, and that few guys are as lucky as I am—to have two fathers who love him."

Gratitude brought tears to Olivia's eyes. "Alex has always been so good to you, so good to both of us."

"And he has wisdom to go along with his goodness."

"Did you thank him?"

"Yeah, and I'm going to Bar Harbor to see him after Dad's home safe and sound."

JAMES OPENED his eyes to total silence except for the monitoring equipment that whirred beside him. Where was he?

He turned his head from side to side, looking for some sign. A nurse smiled at him as she approached his bed.

"Do you need anything for pain, Mr. McElroy?" she asked, her manner brisk and efficient.

"No, I'm okay. It's a little tender, and my chest feels odd."

"But no heaviness?"

"No." He glanced at the water on the table beside his bed.

"Would you like a drink?" the nurse asked as

she finished changing the flimsy sheet they kept over him.

"If you don't mind."

He took a sip from the glass she held for him and lay back down. Everything took so much energy. And then there was the strange confusion he'd been experiencing ever since he'd had the surgery.

Confusion and that damned feeling of vulnerability he'd felt in the past day—or was it two? Whatever number of days, he felt uneasy whenever Olivia left him. The nurse had reassured him that anxiety was normal in his condition.

He watched the nurse leave the room and wondered when he'd see Olivia again. A flutter of air brushed his cheek a moment later, and the door whirred open. Hoping to see his wife's face, he turned his head.

Suddenly Kyle stood at his bedside, an anxious smile on his face. Was he having another dream? Was his yearning for his son becoming part of his mixed-up world? "Hi," he said, not sure of himself at all.

"Dad, how are you?"

Dad? It really was Kyle. His son was here. James fought to keep his voice steady. "Fine. I'm doing just fine."

He needed to tell Kyle so many things. He needed

to have his son sit by his bed and tell him he was coming home to stay. "How was your flight?"

"It was okay, Dad. How are you feeling?"

James drew in a deep breath, feeling his chest catch as he did so, and the wash of anxiety that accompanied it. But it wasn't just the physical pain. *That* he could handle. What if he said the wrong thing to Kyle and his son left him again? Could he risk it? "Did you see your mother?"

"Yes, and she's waiting to see you." He paused. "Mom would do anything for you. Anything at all." Kyle's smile started in his eyes.

He needed to hold his son, tell him how much he loved him. "How long…will you stay?"

"As long as it takes…I have so much to make up for. I should've been here, and when I think of what I said that day…I remember your face. How can you ever forgive me?"

"I forgave you then and there." Seeing the anguish in his son's eyes, James reached for his hand. "It's all over now."

Kyle took his father's hand, his face working to maintain control. "No, it's not. Tell me how I can make it up to you."

James felt the warmth of tears easing down his cheeks. "That's an easy one. Help your mother in any way you can."

"I will, Dad, I will."

OLIVIA WATCHED Kyle as he came into the waiting room. She'd hoped for this for so long, and now that he was here, she was tongue-tied. "How did it go?" she asked, seeing the tight lines around Kyle's mouth.

"It went fine, Mom. He—Dad—looks good, and he seems to be making progress." Kyle sat down beside her and slid his arm around her shoulders.

She leaned closer, drawing comfort from his strength, loving him with all her heart. "I think so, too, but we'll know more when Dr. Crealock examines him. How are you doing? Would you like to go to the house and get unpacked?"

"No, Mom, I want to sit here and talk. Like I told Dad, I'll do anything to make it up to both of you."

Completely happy now, Olivia clung to him. "Oh, Kyle, you're finally home with us. There's nothing more I need."

"I've missed you, Mom."

"Me, too. Your father's going to get better much faster now that you're here."

"So what's been going on? Have you been in this waiting room every day? Would you like to go home for a while, or out for a drive?" Kyle asked.

"Your grandmother sent me home yesterday for a break, so I'm quite happy to stay right here. Would you do me a favor?"

"Sure, Mom."

"When your father and I told your grandmother McElroy about you, she was angry and upset. She still is, in fact."

"Why?"

"It's complicated. She thought she should've been told when you were born. Somehow, she sees that as my fault."

"Even though you and Dad weren't together, and you were married to Alex?"

"Yes. And the next thing she said was that she wanted you to come and see her. We had to tell her you were away, and she blamed James for that."

"And now?"

"He needs to settle some issues with his mother."

"Is Dad willing to do that?"

"I think after this is over, he'll want to do a lot of things differently."

"What about you?"

"I want whatever will make your father's recovery as quick and smooth as possible."

"You can count on me."

"Oh, there you are," Julia said, grinning broadly as she strode across the room. "Kyle, it's so good to meet you."

"Aunt Julia?" Kyle asked, standing up just in time for Julia to throw her arms around him.

"Yes—I'm Julia. Have you seen your father?"

"Yes, I have. He seems pretty good, but he's worried about Mom."

"Those two are hopeless, aren't they?" Julia winked at Kyle.

"Yeah, isn't it great?"

Feeling tears of happiness slip past her eyelashes, Olivia smiled.

CHAPTER NINETEEN

One Month Later

"PUT THAT WHEELCHAIR away," James scoffed as he slid out of the passenger seat. "I'm not an invalid."

"Listen to you. You're Superman, are you?" Kyle chuckled as he helped his father climb out of the car.

James glanced up at his son, and the rush of love nearly knocked his feet out from under him. "I'm so glad you're here, son, and such a help to your mother." How he loved to use the word *son*.

"Oh, I did a few things around the place, but you know Mom," Kyle said as they walked slowly up to the house.

"I'll bet she's waiting just inside the door, wanting to come out and fuss, but knowing I wouldn't want her to think I needed help," James said.

"I *know* she is."

"I'd better look sharp, or she'll come out here, scolding all the way," James said, holding his body straight and tall. "And she'll be on your case for not putting me in that wheelchair."

"Prepare yourself—there's more. She's invited the family for later today. And I'm under strict orders to put you to bed when I get you in the house."

"We'll see about that. I didn't endure all those hours hooked up to tubes to come home and go to bed."

Kyle laughed, and James's spirits rose. To hear his son's voice, to hear him laugh, was everything James could ever have wished for. "Tell you what, why don't we agree that as soon as your mother's done fussing over me, we'll have a little time to ourselves?"

Surprise flitted across Kyle's face.

Oh, hell, had he moved too soon? He and Kyle had had some great chats in the hospital, but not the one conversation they needed to have.

The door swung open, and Olivia moved toward him, her arms outstretched. "You're home!" she cried, a smile transforming her face.

James stopped. In all the years he'd loved Olivia, she'd never looked more radiant, with her dark hair, now tinged with gray, framing her face, and her dark eyes brimming with love for him.

But what moved his heart most was the awareness in those eyes after all this time. "We're here," was the only thing he could say.

He felt his wife's arms go around him, her hands on his shoulders, a catch in her breathing. "I can't believe it."

He stared down at her, at the way her eyes seemed to light up from somewhere deep inside her, the way she looked at him as if there was no one else in her world.

"Do you have any idea how much I've wanted to come home? How many times in the last month I've wanted to make a run for it?" he asked, happiness spreading through him, lessening the anxiety that had been his constant companion in the hospital.

"Do you know how many times I wanted to spring you from that joint?" she asked, the teasing back in her voice, a smile on her beautiful lips.

"Okay, you two, enough of that," Kyle said jokingly, leading the way into the house.

"Maybe you should go up and lie down," Olivia said with a fearful look he'd seen so often in the past few weeks.

But she wouldn't need to look that way anymore. He felt great; his doctor said he was doing fine. From now on, he planned to live his life for those he loved. He was done with being a businessman, and with all the pressures that entailed. He was needed right here.

"No." James held her fingers tight in his grip.

"I'm going to sit down here in our living room. And you're going to make lunch…while we men talk." He traded smiles with Kyle over his mother's head.

Kyle nodded. "Yeah, Mom, we men need private time."

"Well, I guess I know when I've been given my marching orders," she said, a mock frown on her face.

James welcomed Kyle's help in getting comfortable in his favorite chair near the fireplace. "You know, there were a few moments I wasn't sure if I'd make it back to this chair. Of if I'd be an invalid when I did."

James sighed, remembering the evenings he and Olivia has spent sitting by the fire, reading together or simply chatting about the day, their friends or city news. Boston had been home to them after they'd eloped and bought this house. And as much as he wanted to return to Ireland, he wasn't going anywhere for now.

"Mom's sure missed you these past few weeks. I did what I could to make her feel more content, but all she wanted was to see you come through the door. It must be nice to love someone so much. I mean, the way you and Mom love each other is so…I don't know. It's… wonderful."

Kyle looked over at his father, and in a moment of insight, James could see that his son needed to hear about the past.

"Kyle, if I'd had any hint at all that your mother had given birth to you, I would've been there."

Kyle slid into the sofa across from his father, his glance direct. "Why weren't you? Why *didn't* you know?"

"Because I let my parents dictate what I would do with my life. Never once in those early years did I crank up the courage to go to your mother, to try and see her, to know she was all right. Because I was afraid of what my father would do if I tried."

"Mom says that your father threatened her family. Is that true?"

"My father said he'd fire your grandfather Banks if I didn't leave for Ireland. But that shouldn't have stopped me from tracking her down and letting her know I still cared. I did try to find her at Hastings College, to no avail. But mostly I spent my energy on trying to win my father's respect, a pointless task."

"You tried to reach Mom through Gramps and Gram, didn't you?"

"Yes, I did, but they wouldn't tell me where Olivia was. I could hardly blame them. After all, I'd made their only daughter unhappy, threatened their livelihood. What would you or I have done in the same circumstances?"

"I don't know…."

"So you see, the situation made it pretty hard to do the right thing, but I blame myself for what your mother went through."

"I can't allow you to do that," Olivia said, coming into the room.

"Are you eavesdropping?" James asked.

"Only when necessary," she murmured, patting his shoulder on the way to the sofa, where Kyle sat.

"I'm equally responsible for the fact that you didn't know James as your father. But I didn't see it as keeping you from him, I saw it as keeping your life stable. Alex loved you from the first day he saw you and always did everything he could to be a good father. I wanted a home and a family for you, and Alex provided that."

Olivia looked across at her husband. "I've had a lot of time to think about this since you got sick. I believed I was doing what was right for Kyle, but I was really doing it for me—just as Kyle said. I was keeping *my* life stable."

Kyle's expression was horrified. "I should never have said that. I'm so sorry—and I was wrong. The truth is, both of you did what you could to cope the best way you knew how."

"How did we create such a smart son?" James asked quietly.

"I haven't been sitting in Europe all this time without gaining a *little* knowledge. I've had my share of relationships."

"Anyone special?" his mother asked, exchanging a look with James.

"No, no one special. Not yet. Although there's a woman in Scotland I hope to see again...."

LATER THAT AFTERNOON, after a nap that both Kyle and Olivia had insisted on, James sat in the living room reading, while Olivia worked on the daily crossword puzzle. She had her dinner plans underway, and now she waited for her parents to arrive.

"Dad and Mom, there's something you should know," Kyle said, leaning against the door.

"What's up?" Olivia asked, putting down her pen.

"I don't know how you're going to feel about this, but I've been visiting with Gram for the past few weeks."

"Susan?" Olivia asked, glancing at James.

"Yeah. She and I have had a few chats." Kyle rubbed his nose. "She's a lonely woman."

"That's the price you pay when you toss your family out of your life," James interjected.

Kyle turned from one parent to the other. "I hope you're not going to be angry with me, but I invited her over to visit for a while this afternoon."

"You know your mother's invited your other grandparents?" James asked.

Kyle nodded. "But when Gram said yes, I couldn't let her down. And she promised to be on her best behavior."

"Now, *that* I'd like to see," James said.

"Trust me, Dad. After all, I'm an expert in anthropology. Could be she's evolved into a better person."

"Could be you're in for a shock," James countered, but there was no malice in his voice.

"Leave her to me," Kyle said.

What could she say to Kyle? Olivia wondered. Nothing would change how she felt about Susan McElroy, but she'd asked Kyle to find a way for James to reconcile with his mother. And she trusted her son.

"Our very own version of *Guess Who's Coming to Dinner?*" Olivia asked.

"No kidding. Who's responsible for this man who's taken charge of our lives?" James asked with an easy smile. "If you've made any headway with my mother, I'll be surprised."

"I'll go and pick her up, then," Kyle said.

He disappeared out the front door, leaving James and Olivia staring at each other in stunned silence.

"I hope he knows what he's getting himself into," James said.

HER PARENTS had arrived about an hour after Kyle left the house. Her father and James had settled in the den to watch golf on the sports channel, while Olivia and her mother chatted about James's impressive recovery.

For dinner, Olivia had tossed a salad with fresh walnuts and kiwis, and prepared a stuffed salmon for the oven. She was determined that James was going to eat more healthfully than ever. He'd agreed with his doctor for once and finally signed up for an exercise program at the heart institute.

Things would be changing in their lives.

She couldn't believe how understanding and intuitive Kyle had become. Of course, he was a grown man and it was about time, but still, what would she have done without him these past few weeks?

She smiled. Yeah, life was good….

She checked the dining room one more time. The fresh Shasta daisies made a beautiful centerpiece, and the foot-long tapers would set the mood for tonight's celebration dinner.

"Here's Kyle," Edwina said, as she went to the door. "And he has someone with him."

"Susan." Olivia followed her mother.

"The one and only," Edwina muttered.

"It's your mother," Olivia called to James. "She's here."

"And Kyle's helping her out of the car," Edwina added in a disbelieving tone. "What would make Kyle do this? Does he know his grandmother isn't welcome here?"

"Kyle says see asked to see James and me."

Edwina's eyebrows shot up.

"I couldn't say no." Olivia's glance shifted from her mother to Kyle as she watched him wheel his grandmother to the door.

"Your father and I will be in the den if you need us," Edwina said, slipping away.

"Here you go, Gram." Kyle picked her up and carried her into the living room, then put her down in the armchair across from his father.

Susan McElroy looked from Olivia to James, her expression one of uncertainty. Clasping her hands in her lap, she opened her mouth to speak—and closed it.

Kyle knelt beside his grandmother. "Come on, Gram, you can do it."

Susan turned to her son. "I invited Kyle to come and visit me," she said hesitantly.

Kyle glanced over his shoulder at his parents. "I invited myself one day a couple of weeks ago."

"However it happened, we got talking and he reminds me so much of my husband." Her aged hand touched Kyle's arm. "You think they're going to listen to me, do you?" she asked Kyle, her piercing gaze searching his face.

"Like I said, Gram, you've got nothing to lose."

Susan clutched the gold cross that adorned the front of her cream silk blouse. "I want to—to explain what happened that day you came to my house."

Olivia and James looked at each other.

"I want to apologize for what I said." She met Olivia's disbelieving stare.

Could Susan McElroy have changed? Olivia doubted it. Susan had been unbearably rude to her and James, and it just didn't make sense that she could've made such a quick turnaround in her attitude toward them. Olivia gave Kyle a questioning frown.

"I understand how you must have felt, Mom, but I think you should listen to what Gram has to say," Kyle suggested before turning back to his grandmother. "Tell them what you told me."

The room went silent. Susan McElroy worked her fingers through the gold chain around her neck. "I'm lonely," she admitted. "Seeing Kyle makes me remember...so many things. Things I'd change if I could." She glanced at James, but he was looking at Olivia.

"We've all done things we're not proud of," Susan said, returning her gaze to Kyle, a look of love in her eyes that Olivia had never seen before.

"Go on," James said.

"As I started to say, I want to apologize for what I said about Olivia that day at my house."

James shifted in his chair. "You've hurt Olivia in so many ways, and all because you wouldn't take the time to know her. She's my wife, and that's the way it should always have been. How it always *will* be."

She nodded her head ever so slightly. "Kyle helped me see how badly I've acted. Getting to know my grandson has shown me what a fine young man he is, and he tells me it's because he had good parents. And because of me, James didn't get a chance to show how good a father *he* could be"

Susan turned to Olivia. "I should have given you James's number in Ireland. I should have trusted you, and I didn't. I apologize for that, too. I want a chance to start over—if it isn't too late."

Olivia fought back the urge to say some of the things she'd kept to herself all these years. She wanted to vent the frustration and pain she'd suffered because of this woman.

She met her husband's warm gaze from across the room and took a deep breath. "I've loved your son as long as I can remember, Mrs. McElroy. Let me warn you that if you're apologizing in order to get back into our lives to hurt us again, it isn't going to work."

Kyle rose and went to his mother. "Mom, I've spent a lot of time with Gram when you were at the hospital seeing Dad. I told her she'd have to make her apology before the whole family, no private apology or attempt to tell different stories to you and Dad."

"Did you do that for her, Kyle, or for us?" Olivia asked.

"I want to be part of my other family and there's only Julia and Gram now. I want a chance to be part of the McElroy family as well as the Banks family and the Crawfords. Can we give it a try?"

James got up from his chair. "Kyle, your mother and I need a few moments alone."

Kyle nodded.

James took Olivia's hand and led her out to the patio.

"God, how I've missed this house and this backyard with all the roses. Doesn't the air smell sweet?" he asked.

She slipped her arms around his waist and hugged him. "You can skip the introduction. Just get to the bottom line."

"You know me so well," he said, smiling down at her. "Okay, here goes. My mother's sitting in our living room for the first time in her life, waiting for us to forgive her. I can hardly believe it, and I think our son's the one who convinced her to do this. Just because she's here now doesn't mean she's going to be any easier to get along with in the future."

"But James, she's an old woman."

"Don't let her frailty fool you. She's as tough as nails."

"We can't just send her away," Olivia said resolutely. "We have to forgive her, like Kyle said. It's the right thing to do."

"This isn't about my mother or Kyle, it's about you, Olivia. All your life you've done what you thought was right, and kept people in your life because you wanted to do the right thing."

"You're thinking of Alex," she mused.

"And Grace. They're the most obvious ones. But you don't have to do the right thing where my mother's concerned, and certainly not to please me. I want you to know that I'll accept whatever decision you make. My mother and father treated you badly and put every obstacle they could in our way. And you paid the price."

"So did you."

"Not to the extent you did. So if you feel you can't have her in our lives, I'll tell her."

"And what about Kyle?"

"Kyle knows the risk he ran in doing this. It's up to him to decide if he can accept our decision."

What should she do? She had an overwhelming urge to tell the old bat to take a hike. If the tables were turned, she was quite sure Susan McElroy wouldn't forgive *her*. But if she'd been Susan and had risked humiliation to apologize, she'd want a chance to make amends. Didn't Susan deserve this one opportunity?

"James, we may have had a hard time finding our way back to each other, and your mother may be a major cause of the difficulties we had. But I'm so happy to have you here with me, to have our lives and our son. We can afford to be generous, can't we?"

AN HOUR LATER, with everyone gathered around the dining room table, Olivia's heart overflowed with love as she looked down the table, past her parents who sat across from Kyle and Susan McElroy, over the shining white damask tablecloth to where her husband sat.

James met her eyes across the expanse of white linen. And just like that night so long ago, when he'd offered her a ride home from basketball practice, he smiled—and it was as if someone had turned on all the lights.

* * * * *

*Look for LAST WOLF WATCHING
by Rhyannon Byrd—the exciting conclusion
in the BLOODRUNNERS miniseries
from Silhouette Nocturne.*

*Follow Michaela and Brody on their
fierce journey to find the truth and face
the demons from the past, as they reach
the heart of the battle between
the Runners and the rogues.*

*Here is a sneak preview of book three,
LAST WOLF WATCHING.*

Michaela squinted, struggling to see through the impenetrable darkness. Everyone looked toward the Elders, but she knew Brody Carter still watched her. Michaela could feel the power of his gaze. Its heat. Its strength. And something that felt strangely like anger, though he had no reason to have any emotion toward her. Strangers from different worlds, brought together beneath the heavy silver moon on a night made for hell itself. That was their only connection.

The second she finished that thought, she knew it was a lie. But she couldn't deal with it now. Not tonight. Not when her whole world balanced on the edge of destruction.

Willing her backbone to keep her upright, Michaela Doucet focused on the towering blaze of a roaring bonfire that rose from the far side of the clearing, its orange flames burning with maniacal zeal against the inky black curtain of the night. Many of the Lycans had already shifted into their preternatural shapes, their fur-covered bodies standing like monstrous shadows at the edges of the forest as they waited with restless expectancy for her brother.

Her nineteen-year-old brother, Max, had been attacked by a rogue werewolf—a Lycan who preyed upon humans for food. Max had been bitten in the attack, which meant he was no longer human, but a breed of creature that existed between the two worlds of man and beast, much like the Bloodrunners themselves.

The Elders parted, and two hulking shapes emerged from the trees. In their wolf forms, the Lycans stood over seven feet tall, their legs bent at an odd angle as they stalked forward. They each held a thick chain that had been wound around their inside wrists, the twin lengths leading back into the shadows. The Lycans had taken no more than a few steps when they jerked on the chains, and her brother appeared.

Bound like an animal.

Biting at her trembling lower lip, she glanced

left, then right, surprised to see that others had joined her. Now the Bloodrunners and their family and friends stood as a united force against the Silvercrest pack, which had yet to accept the fact that something sinister was eating away at its foundation—something that would rip down the protective walls that separated their world from the humans'. It occurred to Michaela that loyalties were being announced tonight—a separation made between those who would stand with the Runners in their fight against the rogues and those who blindly supported the pack's refusal to face reality. But all she could focus on was her brother. Max looked so hurt…so terrified.

"Leave him alone," she screamed, her soft-soled, black satin slip-ons struggling for purchase in the damp earth as she rushed toward Max, only to find herself lifted off the ground when a hard, heavily muscled arm clamped around her waist from behind, pulling her clear off her feet. "Damn it, let me down!" she snarled, unable to take her eyes off her brother as the golden-eyed Lycan kicked him.

Mindless with heartache and rage, Michaela clawed at the arm holding her, kicking her heels against whatever part of her captor's legs she could reach. "Stop it," a deep, husky voice grunted in her ear. "You're not helping him by losing it. I give you my word he'll survive the ceremony, but you have to keep it together."

"Nooooo!" she screamed, too hysterical to listen to reason. "You're monsters! All of you! Look what you've done to him! How dare you! *How dare you!*"

The arm tightened with a powerful flex of muscle, cinching her waist. Her breath sucked in on a sharp, wailing gasp.

"Shut up before you get both yourself and your brother killed. I will *not* let that happen. Do you understand me?" her captor growled, shaking her so hard that her teeth clicked together. "Do you understand me, Doucet?"

"Damn it," she cried, stricken as she watched one of the guards grab Max by his hair. Around them Lycans huffed and growled as they watched the spectacle, while others outright howled for the show to begin.

"That's enough!" the voice seethed in her ear. "They'll tear you apart before you even reach him, and I'll be damned if I'm going to stand here and watch you die."

Suddenly, through the haze of fear and agony and outrage in her mind, she finally recognized who'd caught her. *Brody*.

He held her in his arms, her body locked against his powerful form, her back to the burning heat of his chest. A low, keening sound of anguish tore through her, and her head dropped forward as hoarse sobs of pain ripped from her throat. "Let me go. I have to help him. *Please*," she begged brokenly, knowing only that she needed to get to Max. "Let me go, Brody."

He muttered something against her hair, his breath warm against her scalp, and Michaela could have sworn it was a single word…. But she must have heard wrong. She was too upset. Too furious. Too terrified. She must be out of her mind.

Because it sounded as if he'd quietly snarled the word *never*.

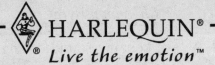

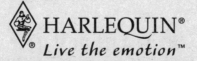

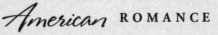
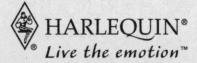

HARLEQUIN®
INTRIGUE®

BREATHTAKING ROMANTIC SUSPENSE

Shared dangers and passions lead to electrifying
romance and heart-stopping suspense!

Every month, you'll meet six new heroes
who are guaranteed to make your spine tingle
and your pulse pound. With them you'll enter
into the exciting world of Harlequin Intrigue—
where your life is on the line
and so is your heart!

THAT'S INTRIGUE—
ROMANTIC SUSPENSE
AT ITS BEST!

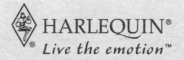

HARLEQUIN®
Live the emotion™

Harlequin® Historical
Historical Romantic Adventure!

*Imagine a time of chivalrous
knights and unconventional ladies,
roguish rakes and impetuous
heiresses, rugged cowboys
and spirited frontierswomen—
these rich and vivid tales will
capture your imagination!*

*Harlequin Historical . . .
they're too good to miss!*